CH00859320

0

RANSOM AND
REVENGE

by Tom Lawson
& Maddy Anderson

To my Grandparents
T.L.

To Nutmeg xxx
M.A.

Contents

Chapter One
The Ins and Outs of the Ridgeways

MR AND MRS Ridgeway sighed as they sat at the dining room table late on a Tuesday evening, pouring over documents. Mr Archie Ridgeway shook his head from time to time as he read on through the paragraphs of words.

He was a tall man, with short curly brown hair, carved features and an interesting nose. His wife, Caroline, however, was a thin woman, with a wide but slightly false smile and elegant pale hands.

The ruffling sheets stopped, the foggy air around them slowed. Both faces looked up, a pen poised between Caroline's fingers.

"How did it go?"

"The money is in the bank and communication has been stopped."

"Are you quite sure?"

"Quite sure."

The tense atmosphere loosened, the shoulders of Caroline and Archie relaxed and the two tall figures, now shadows in the soft glow of a lamp, curved back into their original state, Archie bending to check the document below his eyes one last time.

Around the dimly lit room, pictures of the family were dotted here and there with the perky faces of three children. A mundane creme filled the walls, and not a speck of dirt was to be found upon the tirelessly scrubbed surfaces.

Archie snorted in disgust as he read over the brochure in his hand.

"Darling, I've got to go to bed—it'll be an early start in the morning," piped up Caroline in a cold, strong voice, "and don't stay up too late, remember—you've got to pop into the office before the move tomorrow on top of everything else."

"Yes, you're right, I'll come up in 15," grunted Archie, still studying the pages.

He heard his wife leaving the room, and one minute later, padding upstairs. He murmured to himself, trying to concentrate, as the words started swimming around on the page.

It was no good. He had to get some sleep. Stretching stiffly, he got up from his chair, gathered the endless sheets of paper, and left the room.

It was dark in the corridors, Archie turned on his torch installed on his phone and felt his way through the mountain of cardboard boxes dotted here and there. He was fed up with them, but knew they would all be gone by tomorrow.

Even with everything in boxes, you could tell that the Ridgeway's house was a grand one. Three floors, seven bedrooms, and a large kitchen, many people wondered why on earth they were moving. If she was totally honest with herself, Caroline Ridgeway didn't want to move from their gorgeous stately home, but she knew better than to argue with her husband. He was in charge, he made the decisions. That was that.

The small white light turned off, snapping the room into darkness as Archie crept into the bedroom. He felt his way towards his bed, stretching his arms wildly while gripping at a cupboard or picture frame before slipping his black shoes somewhere under the bed. He then collapsed onto what he hoped was a soft memory foam mattress and, without taking off any of his clothes, slipped in between the silky sheets.

His legs fell almost paralysed onto the bed and his eyes turned unfocused and smudged. Thoughts rushed around his head as a faint smile waved onto his face, the prospect of running further away from that despicable childhood of his gave him a warm sense of pride and belonging. His eyelids pressed shut and not a worry touched his brain as he fell asleep, Caroline still and deadly silent beside him.

*   *   *

The next morning dawned a bright one, the summer flowers finally starting to bloom. A girl with long blond hair and a thin, beaming face sauntered over to the window and looked out. Her face switched from tiredness to delight, it was the first sunny day she'd seen in weeks and was greatly thankful that another day of writing poetry with her brother wasn't in order. She dashed out of her room and into another one, right across the corridor. The room was marked clearly with the sign: Michael's Room.

"Michael!" the girl squealed and a boy with brown hair, who happened to be sitting up in bed. Feeling around, he grabbed his glasses from a box near him and placed them carefully on his nose.

"What is it?" he groaned

"Oh, Michael, look out of the window!"

Michael craned his neck and his eyes flashed firstly to the slightly grey walls, heavily organised wooden desk and finally towards the large, metal framed window.

"I don't see anything exciting, are you wanting to start our poetry lesson early?" he lay back onto his pillows while Penelope gave an obvious roll of her eyes.

"Well then, what is it, Penelope?"

Penelope, who looked ready to jump out of the window herself said,

"Can't you see? It's sunny! We can go and play outside! You, me and Matthew!"

Michael yawned and slowly got out of his bed.

"Now, let me see if I'm free", he stretched, padded over to his desk and started studying the calendar, pinned to the wall.

"Penny! What were you thinking? Of course, I can't play—why today is moving day!" He said looking half shocked, half disgusted.

"Have you done your packing? I finished last night. All that is left is my calendar." and with a smug nod of the head, Michael carefully pulled the glossy papers off the grey wall. He then placed it into his suitcase, and carefully zipped the whole thing shut.

Penelope watched, transfixed before she suddenly exclaimed "Whoops! I haven't even started!" she stumbled back into her room. It was a very different sight. Unlike Michael's, Penelope's walls were covered in things, drawings, posters, and even notes that she'd scribbled down when she had to remember something. The floor was littered in toys and piles of books and bright neon pillows that were sore to the eyes lined her bed.

Penelope's room was not a pretty sight at present however. Though all the members of the family each had their private maids who attended to their rooms 6 days a week, Penelope still managed to get hers in a tip within half an hour of her maid leaving. Michael, who despised all kinds of mess just stayed out of Penelope's room all together these days however he was unable to escape the sign hung up on her door which wrinkled his bones while making him squirm on the few times he forgot to look away.

The sign was awfully gaudy, colours everywhere, with 'Penelope's Room' written in large, bubble letters. Michael very much disapproved when first seeing the sign, but Penelope insisted that it was interesting and he just 'lacked character'.

She was now seizing great handfuls of clothes from her drawers and stuffing them into a large brown cardboard box that stood empty on the floor. She sat crossed legged with a helpless look on her face, overwhelmed at all the clothes she had to put away. She was now beginning to panic as her father had told her to start packing almost a whole week ago.

What followed was pure chaos and mayhem as the family got ready to leave the house. While Michael stood extremely smug by the door, constantly pointing at his watch, Penelope clattered round the whole house snatching at her possessions while giving her brother deadly stares of annoyance. Caroline was also deeply stressed as she swiped different jars and bowls out of the fridge, shoved them into a bag and hurried off to the drawing room. Archie, the children's father had left for the office hours before with a slightly triumphant look upon his face muttering to Caroline about being there at around five.

20 minutes past to find Penelope, Michael and Matthew all packed into their car. The last ten minutes had also been manic

and Penelope had ended up almost sobbing with tears. However, they had got onto the road with five minutes to spare, Caroline in the front, speeding along the motorway. Her face was controlled and blank as it always was. One was never quite sure whether she was thinking or not, whether underneath the passive face ran wild thoughts crashing among her brain.

"Don't push *me*, Matthew!"

"Please can you two boys be quiet?" chirped Mrs Ridgeway, not taking her eyes off the road but clenching her cheek bones all the same.

"It wasn't me! it was Matthew!" Burst out Michael, looking angrily towards a shorter, blond boy, with a round face and brown eyes. Matthew, being the youngest of the family, didn't much like being shoved off by the other two. However, he did like an argument. He was the sort of boy who had too much character. He was also very greedy and liked having his way which didn't do wonders for his spoilt personality.

Matthew rolled his eyes while stretching a rebellious grin, before pulling his eyes towards the window, gazing at the trees as their Porsche slipped off the motorway and made its way along the narrow, slower country roads.

As the smooth, tarmac lane winded round hills and large clumps of bushes, and the grass waved along with fields as far as the eye could see, the children's eyes flickered and flashed along the countryside, anticipation sketched upon their faces. A few hours past and before a crunching, crackle of gravel and shrieks of excitement declared the arrival of the family.

*   *   *

The manor was a large one, with huge electric gates guarding the neat and tidy grounds and a drive leading up to the big front doors which shone navy blue in the afternoon sunlight. Large angled windows stood sharp like hints of what will be seen inside. A ruff red brick carpeted the walls and ribbons of neatly cared for ivy strung themselves upon the wall. Boxes of hedges surrounded the terrace and neat little borders of flowers carved a path to the door.

The children burst out of the car in a wild frenzy as soon as the butler had opened the doors and ran up the steps leading to the great door. They pushed it open and ran inside, leaving their mother to shout at the waiting servants to 'get a move on with the unpacking'.

Caroline hastily slung her bag over her shoulder and swiftly went inside, her red high heels clopping at the pale stone.

"Where would you like these ma'm, in the master bedroom"

Caroline gave a scalding look towards the rough face of the butler, her eyes rolling down to his scruffy black shoes, before giving a tiny nod of consent and pacing forward, feeling a few seconds with that man was quite enough and wanting to check on the children. She found them in the kitchen and showed a modest look around the vast room, her once disgusted face, now arrogant and proud. Matthew was clattering around, opening and shutting cupboards whilst Penelope and Michael shared a smug little smile. Cream coloured shelves lined the walls and duck egg blue drawers formed an island. crystal glasses, large crinkled plates, and tiny espresso cups filled the cupboards and a grand, matured, dark brown table was rooted down onto the tiled and pristine floor. A little antique and wooden bird flew through a hole and a loud few blasts of sound signalled the hour. Caroline snapped to her usual, twisted her back sharply and cast an eye over the children.

"Come along you three, better get unpacking, you'll find your rooms freshly cleaned and your bed dressed in linen. Well, I should hope. That's what I asked *him* to do."

"All right mother." cackled Penelope. "Oh I do hope I have the largest room" she called.

The children removed their shoes and traipsed through a grande entrance room full of polished wooden tables and large, curving ornaments, the smugness gone from Penelope and Michaels faces to reveal an unpleasant expectancy for the butler to bring up a slice of cake. They padded up the large, red-carpeted stairs, taking great care not to trip and started down a similar coloured corridor, several large paintings hanging above their heads. Michael led the way and without warning, darted into a room nearest to the right. Penelope sighed and carried on further, which took her to another large room and Matthew followed suit and barged into a room on the left.

Penelope flopped down on her freshly made bed and gazed at the ceiling wondering what she was going to do. She soon made up her mind and hurried along to Michael's room padding softly at the thick, carpeted floors, much like she had done that morning. She was rather a fan of wandering madly into Michael's room which was not to the liking of Michael.

He was putting up his sign on his door when Penelope approached him. She barged through and went inside the room, finding whitewashed walls and a light brown oak bed. Like Michael, the room was plain, organised, and sensible. Michael obediently and slightly annoyed plodded through behind to find Penelope stretched out on the bed ruffling the sheets either both feet pressed against the pillows. With gritted teeth, Michael pleaded,

"Oh Penny, their brand new sheets and you know how I like my room orderly."

Penelope stretched one final time and flopped off the bed onto the delicate, wooden floor.

"Oh so sorry but do loosen up a bit," she said in a bored fashion.

"Anyway a pity, your room isn't as big as mine although I am the oldest so..." Penelope's voice drowned away.

"Well, I like my room far better than your pink and fluffy disco room." Michael huffed in a disgusted manner.

As he strode over to his desk to check when his tutor would be arriving, Penelope thought aloud,

"I could do it with a glass of water. Well, I'll ring and ask the Butler."

"Yes do and shut the door on leaving because I would like to do some pre-work before my lesson begins"

Penelope got up and headed for the door.

"Oh, you are a big bore. Come down and play a game with me and Matthew, I thought of some chess."

Michael snorted in an unkind manner.

"Well I may be lousy at the game but I can still enjoy myself," she said.

As Michael put down his pen he spoke, "Well yes, I suppose I will come."

Penelope heaved with a sigh. "Good I'll just finish unpacking."

Chapter Two
A Stroll in the Woods

MICHAEL TWISTED THE doorknob and headed downstairs. With his hand gracing a smooth, dark bannister, and his feet ruffling into the scarlet rug below him, his eyes rolled toward a painting of two swans leaping into flight. A shriek from downstairs brought him down to earth and the thought of a game with Matthew who was bound to be competitive struck his mind. He slipped through the door and headed for an armchair mumbling to Matthew about a game of chess.

Penelope, after having shouted at the butler about handling her zebra teddy too roughly, also trotted downstairs, humming a random and slightly out of tune song. She jumped the last few steps and stumbled, but arose and headed for the drawing-room. Upon entering a loud series of squawks meant she had walked in on an argument.

"No I will be white, I am always them in chess." whined Matthew.

"Yes but it's my set, I got it for Christmas!" yelled Michael.

"Oh you two, do be quiet, I could hear you from a mile off!" chirped Penelope.

"Well yes I suppose we were making a racket, let's start." said Michael.

Penelope sat on a puff and handled the chess set onto the oak and glass coffee table. She poured the white and brown pieces onto the table and they clattered. After the setup, Michael crouched to start.

After a hurried game, where Michael had his 200th victory of the year, they decided to go on a walk.

Wellies clattered together, hats and gloves unfolded themselves onto the children's heads and hands, and an umbrella hopped its way out of a pot. The golden doorknob clicked and shut as the children stumbled out onto the beige terrace and the pale green grass. Heavy, grey clouds that almost fell out of the sky started to split signalling a jolly good walk. A soft chatter jumped between the children as they strolled long and wide steps down the muddy path, Matthew jumping in the odd brown puddle.

"Lord this is a wonderful walk, I could almost sing!" Michael tweeted in a sing-song voice.

"Oh please don't I didn't bring my earplugs." sniggered Matthew.

"Rude Matt, rude" huffed Michael.

"I have told you once and i shall tell you again, my name is Matthew, not Matt, not Matty and not any of your other silly names. Matthew." shouted Matthew, his teeth crunching together.

"Alright, keep your hat on, I once heard that nicknames are a great sign of affection." sung penelope. A glare of annoyance met these words so penelope, sensing another argument brewing shut herself up.

They ran in a smart jog across the tarmac, grey road as a bright red BMW slid past. The children gave a hearty wave and a squeal as their father tooted the horn and raced past. They all jumped again and again to see the car and discussed how lucky they were to have the best house on the street.

"Right shall we pop off to the shops?" chirped Matthew.

"Well to be quite frank I find the shopkeeper ghastly so I shan't be," Penelope said dispiritingly.

"Oh you do like to make a fuss penny but well I quite agree. The smell in there wrinkles my nostrils so much that they begin to shake."

The children chuckled in amusement and headed back across the vast fields. Before their eyes lay several empty green canvases waiting for colour. The fields waved like the ocean washing and whipping over their feet. Tall, elegant trees formed around them and a green canopy shaded the three children. Through a few branches, stood a boy crouched with a ruff brown dog in its arms.

The boy had sandy blond hair, blue eyes and was dressed in jeans and a hoodie.

"Oh lord would you look at him, I almost feel sorry for that boy in the intolerable clothes," Penelope said in a disgusted manner.

"Well yes quite and look at that house or should I say shack." sniggered Michael pointing towards a wooden house in the next field.

The children laughed in amusement.

"I'd die if I lived in such a place," roared Matthew. The scruffy clothed boy looked up and frowned, he then bounded off smiling and laughing with his dog who jumped frantically up, ears flailing through the thick hair, trying to reach his face.

As the children then strolled through a vintage wooden gate with detailed metal bolts, they peered over at the gardeners who seemed to at that moment be chatting to one another.

Mr and Mrs Pot, who were sodden with sweat and wiping a red arm among their foreheads at that moment, were an old fashioned but kind couple. Mrs Pot's wrinkled, dry and slightly grubby face although not being the cleanest, held a warm and wide smile and bright blue eyes that shone just above her cheeks seemed to act like a torch to the surroundings. In contrast to this Mr Pot was a short but plum-shaped man with a portly belly and thick, sturdy legs. He wore large leather wellingtons and a loose chestnut belt filled with shovels and spades hung around his hips. His face wore a grumpy and disheartened look and his hair was scruffy holding twigs and soil.

"Excuse me but do you mind not talking and actually gardening?" sighed Penelope, interrupting their conversation.

"Yes I would like those potatoes for dinner you know," said Michael.

"They could even be the mother and father of that boy in the forest looking at the state of their clothes." chuckled Matthew.

"Now that's a bit unkind, children, you up for a job digging the carrots?"

Three puzzled and horrified looks greeted these words and they spluttered about how they were not to be treated as slaves and would never lend a hand to such a *physical* job. The children stalked off in an unkind manner leaving Mr Pot to shout insults at the children and Mrs Pot feeling hurt. They trooped inside, with their toes sore and legs tired and collapsed into the drawing-room among the puffed-up squashy red armchairs.

Archie drove into his impressive drive with a slight grin etched onto his face. He had done it. He couldn't be called poor anymore. All Archie's childhood, he had been laughed at, told he wouldn't achieve anything, been the worst of the worst.

"Well." he muttered to himself.

"I've proved them wrong."

But, instead of the happy feeling that he'd been expecting, a clench in his stomach reminded him about how far he needed to go, but for now he was happy. He must be happy. The house he was about to walk into was the grandest of grand. Was the best on the street. No one could look at him and see that poor, distasteful childhood in his past.

The car door clapped shut, a crackle of gravel crinkled under Archie's feet and a herd of black birds fled into the sky. His eyes fell mesmerised onto the large house, the smart garden and the clipped flowers that stood sharp in a few brown pots. A small chuckle was released from Archie's wide smile, the pang of anger dissolving into nothingness. He grazed his long fingered hands along the red BMW, met the back seat handle and pulled the door open, then slid his arms into the car and heaved out a polished slab of wood, before placing it carefully under his arm.

Archie swiftly strolled, still smiling, to a stone wall, grabbed a few long, metal nails from his pocket as well as a hammer and slapped the board to the sandy, red bricks. He hammered and banged for a good few minutes until finally standing back. Ridgeway Manor was written in long, golden letters and sparkling in the evening sunlight. An arrogant snigger pressed upon his face and he strode slowly and confidently towards the door grabbing at his phone. His hand lay, gripping the doorknob as he whispered.

"Another sale, what a lucky family, or at least until they see what they have bought."

The door closed.

*   *   *

A puzzle sat with its colourful pieces shining haphazardly across the dining room table and the children's eyes rolled from side to side slowly examining and searching for pieces. The room was silent with Caroline deep in an Agatha Christie book, her legs crossed on an armchair. The only sound and movement to be heard was the new cook bustling around the kitchen, two saucepans gripped into her stubby, greasy and wrinkled fingers, and sodden clothes being flung into the vast blue washing basket by the butler. A faint crackle of gravel was heard and the children swirled into motion running to the front door. There stood their father, tall and proud while holding a new mobile phone in one hand. Penelope, transfixed, immediately headed straight for the phone having completely forgot about her father's return. She raced back to her mother to leave the other two to greet their father into the kitchen.

The evening ended with Matthew and Penelope curled up on a sofa watching tv while Michael clutched a book trying to ignore the sound from the program they were watching. Penelope heaved a sigh and shrieked for the butler to run a bath. He swiftly paced in and stood to wait for instruction as Penelope sighed:

"Butler, do run me a bath and make it hot. I want to be warmed up, not cooled down like I did last time!"

"Yes and make my bed, I want linen sheets tonight," Michael said, raising his eyes from the flaking pages in annoyance. There was no doubt about it. Michael liked a good book.

As light by light went out along the corridor Caroline tiptoed through, her eyes unfocused. One could tell she, while never showing it, had worries to think about herself. She drifted through the grey toned walls and elegant glass dressing table of her bedroom into her white, almost blinding bathroom. She stared into the mirror, her long breaths clouding up the reflecting surface. All was well, mostly.

Chapter Three
A New House, a New Life

BY THE NEXT morning the children, as well as the servants, had thoroughly settled into their new home. A light breeze rippled through the open windows and swirled around the rooms creating wafts of fresh daisies and mown grass around the house. Mrs Ridgeway was already in the kitchen, enjoying her morning cup of coffee as she looked at the magazines gathered in a new pile on the table. She had already said her farewells to Mr Ridgeway, who had left when it was still dark out.

Mrs Ridgeway thought of her childhood home, she wondered what they were doing now and whether they missed her, it had now been almost 15 years since she'd walked out, a young fiancé to Archie. Caroline sighed and turned back to the magazines, trying to immerse herself back into the world of celebrities and forget her past life no, that was the past, she had tried to visit her family almost 5 years ago, but Archie had disallowed it, it wasn't surprising considering he forbade her to even keep in contact with them ever since the incident where her mother had confronted Archie about them marrying so soon.

After a while, Caroline heard footsteps overhead. It sounded like a herd of elephants, so she assumed that it must be Penelope or Matthew, Michael would never walk like that. A few moments later and she heard them all plodding downstairs and braced herself by taking a large gulp of coffee, she wasn't going to have the children see her so wistful, no, she would be strong and in control of her emotions at all times.

A few moments later, the youngsters burst through the door, chatting about the new film that they had seen for Matthew's birthday a few months back, the wizard of Oz.

"Good morning children!"

"Morning mother" came the automatic acknowledgement that was repeated every morning.

"Oh, do come and sit down, darlings"

They did as they were told, Penelope quicking her pace to get to the spot she always liked, with the bright pink plate settled on the white tablecloth.

When the children were settled at the table, Caroline passed them all the big large platter, today, it was piled high with luscious French toast, the children's favourite, not made by Caroline of course but credit had been taken all the same. As the plate slowly emptied, cups having been drained by the children, the conversation turned to Caroline, the usual topic of what her and Archie's job consisted of returning once again .

"Your father and I work in the house developing and selling industry" Caroline squeaked in a very formal voice.

"And let I tell you now, houses are flying off the shelves, it really is like growing a money tree in the back garden."

The Butler stepped lightly in and stood by the table awaiting the picking up of plates. Penelope with a smug glance at the butler said,

"That surely must be why we can afford such a grand house!"

"Yes, it must be, oh I do love it," agreed Michael.

A chatter of voices started up as the children gloated over their favourite rooms in the house.

Suddenly, like the blade of a knife into bread, the Butler bent forward.

"May i take a plum,"

The room went silent and even the cook froze with a jug of orange juice in one hand. Caroline shook her head slowly before ever so slightly opening her mouth.

"Just one plum?"

"Yes, one plum madame."

A whisper broke out between the children of how rude the butler was being and how these kinds of action would not be tolerated. After a very long pause, Caroline said clenching her jaw in a strained and reluctant voice

"Yes, you may have one plum, but eat it in the washing room, I don't want you here."

Butler stretched his hand and picked up a plum, the children's eyes following his grubby hands in horror. He then strolled out towards the washing room to a chorus of tutting from the children.

*   *   *

Archie strolled meaningfully through two large double doors and gave a sharp push on the up button. The doors slid open and he strode into the lift. Thoughts of his two new sales burst into his brain as the slow rise of the floor flew him towards the sky.

He pulled out his office chair and sat down unlocking his 16 digit password.

After two hours passed full of emails and documents Archie was found twisting his car key and driving off towards the edge of the city. A sharp crack of gravel and a puff of smoke from the car meant Archie had arrived at the house. With his fingers sliding and tapping on his phone swiping to find the photo he had posted of the house he strolled down the dirty, dusty, grey drive to a small wooden shack-like house with broken windows and peeling walls. He stepped cautiously up the front steps which were cracked and broken, and smugly smiled around looking at the old plastic kitchen and the garden table and chairs, A sharp 'Ha' from Archie broke the silence and he sniggered,

'Another lucky family."

A ping from his pocket distracted Archie and he pulled out his phone to look at an email from a certain Richard Dornman. It read 'will see you in the office for the exchange. Thanks a million. Richard.'

The car door slammed and he raced across the country roads. He quickly flicked his eyes to his mobile phone texting Caroline about the new sale and switched on the radio, a wide smile having spread upon his face.

Caroline perched upon the grand kitchen island ruffling through emails on her modern and new computer. Her eyes shone square revealing the hours she had spent behind that screen as her pupils darted across the endless lines of words. Her thin and elegant legs shook slightly as a vibrating phone signalled a message. She reached into her pocket and pulled out a phone to reveal a text from Archie. She smiled as she saw that her husband had cheated another person out of money but a flutter of butterflies burst into her stomach as the thought of the anger in their clients' faces. She confided this feeling with Archie as she knew he would know what to say and tapped a reply before wearily clawing her eyes back onto the screen. Another day passed for Caroline, with her family, a distant memory. Oh, she so wished to have them back in her life, to see them one more time.

Chapter Four
Posh And Spoilt: That's The Ridgeways

THE BUTLER RAN into the hall, gasping for breath. He had done it. He had overslept past his three o clock alarm again! He scurried into the hall, turning up all the hearth rugs as he went, his small eyes darting here and there, checking to see if he had been spotted by a beady stare from the keeper, or even worse, one of the children. He might be turned out onto the street, his family would have no one to provide for them—Samuel was still grieving for his wife who had passed away in childbirth to his 4-month-old twins. He ran his fingers through his unwashed and hastily combed back hair, stooping, he stopped to pick up a crisp £50 note that had been carelessly left by one of *those* children. What wouldn't he have given to be able to pick up that note, which would provide his family with all the necessities they would need for over a month. He glanced around. Annie, the scullery maid was eyeing him suspiciously and he knew, if he took that note, she'd have the house onto him in a jiffy. He placed the money on the nearest table, straightened up and walked out of the hall—his family didn't need riches and servants—they were happy already, or that's what he told himself.

*   *   *

A stiff, tall man with glasses atop his nose strode up the driveway from his small grey car into the overhanging shadow of Ridgeway Manor. His eyebrow ruffled as Michael opened his window just above his head and yelled out something about practising algebra.

Mr Harris, although known to the children as 'The Tutor', sighed, wondering whether Michael would be as needy and bratty as the day before. The shout from the window seemed to answer this question already. He went up the stairs, giving a short wave to Caroline, which was not returned and headed into the nursery (where the children did their lessons) to find Michael's face eagerly waiting for his arrival.

The nursery was a wonderful room, a colossal dolls house, large enough for two children to fit inside took up a whole corner of the place. The walls were dressed in a pale plum and were littered with shelves that were stacked with dolls, teddies and books. A large window took up nearly a whole wall and a blackboard rested before three tables and chairs which were a full shade of brown. Michael's favourite colour.

Michael so loved his lessons and respected his tutor almost as much as his father, which said a great deal. Penelope and Matthew were more interested in the talking of the toys that were stored in the boxes, still not unpacked to even acknowledge Mr Harris' stern face, but quickly slid into their desks and sat behind the blackboard at the sound of his fake cough.

Penelope slouched in her desk in the nursery, baffled. She glanced around and looked at Michael, scribbling down something or other for all he was worth. She twisted around to stare behind her and looked at Matthew, who was busy drawing a spaceship on his maths paper blasting around a few sums. Mr Harris floated up to her and, in a raspy voice asked subtly if she would require some help. Her face burning, Penelope bent her head over her Latin textbook, pretending to study the verbs.

Finally, for Penelope and Matthew, a gratefully warm lunch arrived. Michael looked downright disappointed at the end of the session and, after marking his place in his geography textbook, slipped it into his desks drawer, vowing to read it after lunch. Mrs Dandy, the cook, shuffled in with a platter of sandwiches. The children wheeled across to the table on their spin chairs with their legs dragging across the floor and tucked into the steaming thick soup and egg and pickle sandwiches

*   *   *

A knock at the door interrupted Mr Harris' second lecture on the proper way of answering $3x + 2y = 4$. Penelope screeched and jumped up—she had been bored out of her wits for the past 20 minutes. Matthew hurried along after her and Michael heaved his body from the chair, a disappointed smile stretched upon his face once again, and plodded down the stairs looking apologetically at the tutor.

With a dramatic heave of the door, Penelope pulled it open and stood stock still awaiting the reasoning for the knock. A tall young fellow grinned down at her whilst gripping a large cardboard box that had the words FRAGILE and FIRST CLASS stamped in large red letters on every side. The man, who must have been about 19 or so, was looking around as though he had never seen such a place, his blue eyes scanning the gardeners and the woods beyond. Penelope bounced out and gabled at him. "Oh is this for us?"

"Probably sent on by Father" added Michael,

"he's *always* doing these sort of things".

"I assume yer two are in charge of this parcel then?" Put in the watching delivery man, "do yer want me to set it up then?"

He narrowed his eyes and looked down the passageway behind the children, clearly wanting to see what riches this house held.

"Oh no, we've got a Butler for that." Added Michael with a sneer.

"Well, yer two are lucky to have such a large television set."

"Three! There's three of us, only Matthew went to play trains I think."

"Yes and Mother and Father work hard at their job so this is theirs"

"And ours!"

"Yes, Penny, and our reward."

The delivery man looked the children up and down, staring at their gold wristwatches, taking in they're fine clothes.

"Well, you best be off then," Michael said bossily

"and *don't* mark the patio with that hideous van."

*   *   *

After reasoning for the last 15 minutes with Caroline that he should get his one free evening off a year, Samuel Wilkinson, the butler, stretched his legs and collapsed into a steady walk down the road. He pulled his sweaty and uncomfortable jacket off his back and ruffled the white shirt which puffed up with fresh air sending a satisfying sensation down his backside. He trudged into the ruff muddy track lined with huge, clay filled ruts and leapt over the wooden fence towards a small orange lit barn. He sighed with relief and shuffled through the door into a small and dark wooden room. A large brown plank on top of stilts stood in the middle of the room with DIY haphazard-looking cupboards lining the walls. A soft yellow glow, however, created a cosy and warm atmosphere and created large shadows from the cracked stone tiles that carpeted the floor. His children were huddled together, covering themselves with a thin, grey blanket and trying to comfort the two babies. Samuel's oldest, Luke, was desperately trying to share his body heat with his younger siblings as much as he could. He knew what his father's workplace was like, and how hard he worked, so tried to keep his worries to himself. One of his new siblings, one of the ones that had caused his beloved mother's death, cried and Luke automatically rocked her in his arms before setting her down and walking towards his father.

"Hi dad, how was your day?" Luke asked, already knowing the answer

"The same. I'll get by, son."

"I wish you could quit—then we could be a family"

"Yeah," Samuel forced a smile

"but we'd be a hungry family"

Luke ran forward and hugged his father round the middle. His lack of love and childhood seemed to have stunted his growth so he was shorter than the average 11-year-old.

Samuel peeled them apart after a few seconds and sat him down on the blanket, before kissing him on the forehead.

"Right you three off to bed, common I'll take you up" The four children who, by wearing greying, rough clothes and no shoes, looked like the opposites of the ridgeways headed upstairs and Luke placed the babies into their cots. After the kids lay quietly in one small cave-like room Samuel ducked under the low ceiling into his bedroom and slumped heavily into his bed. His eyes began to close as the thought of finally leaving that house entered his mind. Luckily he fell asleep before the thought of how this would never happen returned. For now, the family although not the richest, lay asleep and happy.

*   *   *

Caroline was strolling down early in the morning to the kitchen for a short walk when a loud clang of metal smashed at the ground. She shrieked and crossed down to find the cook frozen staring at the saucepan. Caroline burst out fuming.

"Right that is, get out, you are dismissed. First not buying the food meaning I have to get it and now you have woken up the whole house.

"Um, sorry" Mrs dandy whimpered

"Oh shush. That's it I'm going on a walk and I want you packed and gone by the time I return."

She stormed out the door and one again howled at the butler for being late by 2 minutes. The butler shuffled to see Mrs dandy crying into her tea towel and ran to comfort her but there was nothing he could do. Her days at this house were over.

As the clock struck 10 oclock Archie was to be found stiffly sitting in the car, a steering wheel in front of him and the engine off. His eyes were narrowing upon an email on his phone distracted from the crowds of people shoving past to the shops which would have annoyed Archie greatly in normal circumstances. His eyes crossed from side to side glinting in anger as his cheeks reddened. He was waiting for his wife. Caroline trotted with a shopping basket hanging loosely in her arm across the isles of the supermarket. She snatched at a packet of pasta and grabbed at two red apples. Her face was screwed up in annoyance in having to do the shopping when normally the butler of some other member of staff would be attending to it. After having a full-on row with the shopkeeper about the change she was meant to receive she headed out clopping into a jog. Caroline was a rich woman but would always get the money she deserved. Her eyes widened in worry that Archie would be angry at the amount of time spent in the supermarkets and flung a basket onto the pile looking back in disgust at the crowded and grubby supermarket. The car key twisted and a loud rev started the car. As the smart couple speeded along the highway caroline leant to turn the music on but Archie quickly held her hand back and said

" Listen caroline, I got an email from one of my clients about wanting his money back."

Caroline's eyes bulged in horror but just kept her face on forcing a calm ok.

" it could be seen as a threat, but this has happened many other times, so I'm not worried"

Caroline whispered in a forced voice

"Read me the email"

Archie protested but in the end, caroline got her way and with his eyes, on the road he reached for his phone and started to read

"This is the last email he has sent me. Sir ridgeway, may I remind you again that I want my money back and I will get it. I warn you revenge will come and soon, look after your family Archie as well as yourself."

Carolien clutched at the car seat and scrunched her face trying to keep calm. She would keep strong and relaxed around Archie. She sat still in silence but inside screams filled her head as worries raced around. Archie drove on saying

"It will be ok, I'm not worried."

Chapter Five
A Butler's Struggle

AS THE EARLY evening arrived, Samuel was still heated with the way Mrs Ridgeway had treated Mrs Dandy, he thought it was unreasonable and that she had only dropped a pan. But that was the Ridgeways. His ideas to just quit strengthened and he was not feeling in the mood to set up another game with the children or bring them another pointless glass of water. The telephone rang like a shrill banshee through the empty house. Samuel scurried through the passageway towards the machine.

He picked up the receiver

"Ridgeway family Butler speaking, who is it?"

"You may not know me" came a soft reply. The voice was silky smooth but sent shivers down Samuel's back all the same.

"Anyway, is this Samuel Wilkinson?"

"Yes…"

"Do you by any chance know of the Ridgeway's?"

"Err yes I am their butler at their new house," Samuel replied tentatively. He had never had a phone call like this before. People who called never asked him these personal questions.

"Would you say they are pleasant people, kind, even generous?"

Samuel looked around. Tell the truth and risk being sacked or lie.

"Samuel?"

Glancing around Samuel lowered his voice and in a hoarse whisper said "No sir, not at all, they're rude, selfish and spoilt."

"Do you realise that Mr Ridgeway has stolen 2.1 million pounds from my possession?" The voice rose in anger and the speaker seemed to be trying to calm down.

"No sir"

"I want revenge, Samuel. I want my money back—will you help me?"

"I'd lose my job, my family, I...I -"

"Samuel I could give you a job in my company, if you do this, I could grant you whatever you please, I could provide for your family, if you help me you shall be the winner in the end."

"What do you want me to do?" whispered Samuel, after a pause.

"I want you to find a way to bring the three children into my possession"

"KIDNAP? We're going to *kidnap* the children?"

"Well." The voice sounded menacing now, "let us call it a short stay, a holiday, do you agree?"

The Butler gulped.

As rain lightly spotted onto the grey tarmac road and car lights blazed splashing the pavements, the children zipped up their hoods on the way back to Ridgeway manor. The tutor's car had not been working so the children had to walk over to his house. They were annoyed and bad-tempered.

"Why should we walk over to his house in this grim weather" wind Matthew

"yes it's horrific, I would rather not have lessons than a walk in this ghastly weather," said Michael

"ditto" barked Penelope.

The three children strolled long wide steps staring at the ground trying to avoid the rain. They turned into the drive and saw that red BMW that meant father was home. They shrieked and ran in to meet their father. "oh I bet he's got something new for the house"

They barged through the large front door to find Archie pulling off his crisp velvet jacket while chatting swiftly to Caroline. His hand lay proud on top of two large cardboard boxes with his long twig-like fingers curled over the corner of it. The three children took a double take from Archie to the boxes before rushing toward it and quickly pulling apart the box, greeting their father as they did so.

Half an hour past to find Penelope slumped in a turquoise velvet armchair spreading her arms onto the armrests. Michael stood tall beside her, his arms crossed and an annoyed look on his face

"it's my turn penny, now get off"

"Oo and me next"

said Matthew who was currently leaning over the back of a new sofa.

"Oh do wait for Michael, father I love them, now I can sit on new chairs in front of a new television"

The children and Archie bustled around the new furniture looking inquiringly at all the buttons and patches. Caroline burst into the room looking fit too burst to eye her watch.

"Your three-bed, it's half-past nine"

"Oh lord is it, good night mother" called Penelope in a sing-song voice

Yes, good night father, love you" said Matthew softly.

"Yes yes," Archie said absently concentrating on his phone. The children stomped up the stairs and once again automatically spun into each of their rooms.

A breakfast table lay full and grande on the long brown oak surface as the children skipped in after an early game of racing demon.

"And it seems I have won again," said Michael

"Oh Michael, nobody cares, it is just a game" whispered Penelope although she did wear an annoyed face. Food of all types lay in platters and bowls in front of the children. Croissants, fruit salads, pancakes and all, spread wide, giddy smiles upon Matthew, Michael and Penelope's faces. It seemed the new cook was a huge success.

A day of documentaries, board games and a few long arguments between the children followed and by the evening the three children were in particularly bad moods. It was a delicious hot meal for supper but the table lay quiet, the sound of knives and forks clattering filling the large kitchen. The plates lay clean with the odd crumb of shepherds pie and Caroline started up

"Children, the butler has set up a game in the drawing-room, run along and start"

"Oh lord what fun, I do hope it's a monopoly" squealed Penelope

"oh no, that takes hours," said Michael.

The children rushed into the old fashioned, vintage drawing room with a tree's worth of reflecting wood stretching all of eight metres across the room. Patch panels of oak tiled the walls and a large tapestry which was full of colour and intricate patterns of some historic event were strung onto one wall. The butler was carefully clicking in train railway pieces. A long track with the odd train on top ran circling, turning and swerving around the table. the children squealed in excitement and pounced towards the trains their eyes flashing from bridge to tunnel. Yes, some would say that 12-year-old children are too old for trains but as you will see the Ridgeway children were not normal and luckier than most.

"oh lord, something else that is new"

"yes, imagine having the same old teddy every day," Matthew said in repugnance

The butler backed away from the table absentmindedly clearly deep in thought, emotion running wild inside his small slightly wrinkled head that showed a small shining bald patch.

Archie and Caroline, we're left to themselves and with a glass of deep scarlet wine tinkering on the table, Caroline said slightly nervously

"I suppose you think they were empty threats"

"Oh yes, of course, you worry too much dear, what harm can they do"

he swallowed.

"yes I suppose your right, let's go and watch the children"

Caroline whimpered and crept off slightly shakily. Archie gulped down the wine and watched her walk away with a touch of worry in his mind but wiped it away and strolled on after her.

Archie left to do some night time business to leave Caroline once again on her own. Though she had a massive house, a husband and three children she seemed to find herself alone a lot and didn't quite know why. She sat on her bed, her hands gripping the linen duvet and her thoughts once again returned to her family. Her two sisters and her mother and father. Was there an ounce of regret in her head? She pulled herself up and walked to a vast wardrobe where under piles and piles of clothes she reached out a small frame with five fair people all smiling up at the camera. A small weep jumped from her mouth and she instantly felt ashamed. But with a bit of confidence injected into her, she pulled it out and rushed to put it on her bedside table. A few tears fell onto her cheek and she sat staring right at the picture. A knock at the door snapped her back to reality and she swiftly wiped her tears from her slightly reddened cheeks. Matthew walked in and strongly said

"Mother, have you seen my pyjamas?"

like the click of a switch, she swirled into her original character

"Oh no I haven't dear, no doubt the butler has misplaced them, give him a shout."

" all right" Michael answered and padded out onto the landing with a wide yawn.

Chapter Six
A Plan In Action

IT WAS A bright morning at the Dornman house. A small family of three lay in their beds, Richard and Harriet quietly chatting about the day ahead. Their house was a fair one with bright flower beds crisscrossing around the garden and a long lawn stretching about 50 metres behind. White walls and wooden panels lined the house and large glass windows and doors were spotted along the walls. With just a look at the village, you could tell it was a friendly one. A little corner shop with bunches of flowers either side of the door sat opposite their house and a few groups of people chatting enthusiastically while off to the shops or the pub or even to each other's houses. Signs of fun chess clubs and yoga classes fluttered on walls and a trickling river ran across the side of the pavement.

One eight-year-old child with combed-back hair, a neat collared shirt and a brown bubbly face named Oscar sat perched at the kitchen island, his cheeks stuffed with rice Krispies. His mother Harriet strolled in with a roll of wrapping paper and a pair of scissors in her hand.

"You've got that birthday party this afternoon, it's Aaron's." She said in a kind but strong voice.

"Oo, what are we getting him?"

"I thought a frisbee would be nice, I'll just wrap it now."

"Ok cool." Oscar said in an offhand voice. Harriet started to slide her scissors across the smooth paper and folded it to wrap around the circular box. Richard Dornman walked down the stairs and crept over to kiss his son on the top of the head. He was a tall and muscular man with a serious face. One could tell he had a dark past and was trying to forget it and become a better person, but instincts had to occur. He picked up a green and thick smoothie off the island and lightly kissed Harriet before waving his goodbyes and running out of the door.

"I'll be meeting Archie Ridgeway about the house this afternoon." Richard said and a shadow covered his face, unnoticed by his wife. "And I won't be here this weekend, a tiresome business trip has just come up"

"Oh, well all right, come home as soon as you can," Harriet said, raising her head to look up into her husband's face from her wrapping. The door shut and Max pushed himself off the stool and ran into the playroom.

*   *   *

The Ridgeway's house once again stood quiet and still equalling for another dull day. As the clock struck 7 in the evening and supper was done, Michael was to be found perched on his neatly made bed deep in a book as per usual.

The sun was just setting when Penelope barged once again into Michael's room. The growth that followed had been repeated about twenty-five times that week as Penelope had come into his room at least two times a day. She slouched onto the bed and started fiddling with the sheets.

"Penny, what are you doing on my bed, can't I have one room to myself?" pleaded Michael

"Sorry Michael, I'm just looking for my book, but let's talk, I'm tired of our parents"

Penelope picked herself up from the bed and walked to Michael's desk before starting to spin on Michaels chair.

"Oh if you must." Said Michael, cringing.

The two started to chat, Penelope enthusiastically and Michael slightly tiredly. Topics of the tutor, the house and the parents came up before Penelope decided she wished for a bath and called:

"BUTLER!"

"Yes coming," said Samuel slightly annoyed but also with a spark of excitement in his eyes. Penelope stretched widely and left wishing Michael a short goodnight and Michael neatly unfolded a corner of his duvet and slithered in determined to keep the bed made.

As the stars slowly flashed into the dark blue blanket of the sky and dark hills looked across the skyline, the rain started to slowly spit against the double glazed windows. the three children lay still under their thick, fluffy blankets and duvets asleep, full to the brim of food and happy. Archie and Caroline stepped ghostly up the stairs ready for an early morning meeting with a new client in London and glided into their large bathroom equipped with double sinks, a large, white tub and golden plated taps. They automatically brushed their teeth and collapsed into bed, their eyelids slowly drifting downwards as sleep waved upon them.

By eight o'clock in the morning the butler had already haphazardly shuffled in with shopping bags swinging around his waist and Archie and Caroline had marched out of the door, a slim black case tightly gripped in their hands. The Children, however, were just beginning to awake, sleep dust crackling along with their eyelids.

As they trotted down the stairs animatedly chatting cheerfully, the butler crept in and with a faint smile said

"Children, your mother and father have asked if you would like to come outside and see a new present they have got, do you want to come"

"Lord almighty, yes" Michael shrieked with the other two sending a chorus of inaudible but joyful sounds across the corridor.

"Then come outside with me, we will have breakfast afterwards," he said, leading the children to one of the many back and side doors leading from the house. The children agreed and swiftly followed taking the odd jump and skip in excitement, their faces lit and eyes wide with joy. They were very eager and started to push around the butler not noticing the grimace upon his face. He clicked the door and opened it wide releasing the children like hounds counting forward in a race.

"A car!"

"A new red car" the children breathed in awe

"Oo how exciting, I'll be driving it first of course," said Penelope and she continued to babble pure nonsense about when and where she would drive. As this happened Michael and

Matthew went to pull the door so excited by the colour that they didn't focus on who was in it. As the butler stealthy remarked

"Have a try sitting inside, a brand new type of leather I here"

The children shuffled inside gasping at how soft the seats felt. Suddenly in a burst of sound and movement, Samuel slammed the doors, the children screamed, and a grunt of excitement came from within the car. Once again the children gave a double-take from the slammed door to the front seat. While all this was happening Samuel whirled into the front and the engine started. A smooth reverse turn signalled a last look at Ridgeway Manor. The car slid onto the road, the three childrens horrified silent screams in the back and a triumphant grin upon the faces of Mr Richard Dornman and Samuel. The now former butler of the ridgeway house.

Chapter Seven
Oh, What To Do?

THE CHILDREN WERE being shoved into a dark room, by rough, masculine hands. Penelope was shrieking indignantly "Get OFF me!"

"Let go of us at ONCE" added Michael, his usually calm tone of voice rising a few octaves.

"Yes" put in Matthew, thinking he'd better add in something,

"my father will hear about this!"

"Don't think you'll have your job any longer Butler!" Shouted Penelope. She then stopped, looking at a dark figure, "Who are you?"

The dark figure moved forwards.

"Get inside that room now and stay there. I am holding a gun so don't mess around with me."

"You need a license for that!"

"Shut UP Penny, this is serious"

"Oh jolly well stop telling me what to do Michael!"

"Right get in, all of you."

Matthew whimpered in fright and clutched Michael.

"Just do what he says Penn," muttered Matthew under his breath.

"Well if you're calling ME Penn I think I can call you -"

The butler grabbed the three of them and shoved them in the dark dingy room. Richard slammed the door shut and pressed his full weight onto it as he turned the key.

"You three stay in there and don't make a sound, or you will regret it. If you knew what your parents had done to me, you would want revenge too. Don't attempt to escape or struggle or you'll have the point of my gun to answer to."

Behind the closed door, Matthew grabbed hold of Michael's hand—he had never liked the dark.

"Penny where are you going?" Inquired Michael, ignoring Matthew's grip on his paw.

"Just exploring" came Penelope's careless reply, "wait! There are stairs here!"

Michael cautiously flipped a switch to reveal a yellow glowing lamp that created long dark shadows that drifted around the room. Two or three wooden boxes with large red stamps printed onto them stood in one corner and an old brown broom stood precariously against a few ruff red bricks. Thick blankets of grey, fluffy dust sat heavily on the floor and the children watched in disgust as a blow of wind set off a cloud of dust. The odd stick and pebble sat sad and dull on the floor and a few tiny claw footprints were seen on the uneven slabs of stone. They slumped depressed and confused, huddling in a corner in silence. Penelope sat against the wall, her legs wide and long stretched out onto the cold floor. Michael crouched refusing to get dust on his clothes and Matthew was shrivelled up leaning against Penelope's shoulder. Although not a sound was shared between them, the same thought of what they were going to next flowed between them.

By the evening, the shock of being kidnapped had sunk in and the children sat put out and worried wondering what they were to do.

"Mother and father surely will come back for us"

Said Matthew hopefully

"Yes definitely, they love us," said Penelope convincingly and Michael nodded his head in agreement. "Although I hope we get supper, it's been several hours, I was expecting lunch but nothing"

A thick metal door was heaved slowly outwards and in came Samuel holding one faded spotted tray full of small, plastic, creme bowls with lumps of god knows what in one hand and a script and piece of paper in the other with a passive look on his face. He stepped down and smashed the tray onto one of the boxes clearly liking his authority over the little monsters.

"Right, Matthew come into the corner now"

"What, I don't think I should be taken orders from a butler" he spluttered in alarm,

"Just do it, Matt, then we might get out of here"

Said Michael in a soothing voice

"Umm Mathew and well all right" obviously Matthew was still oblivious to what was happening.

"Matt, just shut up and do it," Penelope called in A parrot-like voice. He did as he was told and was shoved aggressively by the script and crumpled piece of paper by Samuel. Richard dornman clumped down looking grim but slightly proud with a large iPad gripped tightly in his long and stiff fingers.

"Read this when I say and hold this up," said Samuel menacingly. Matthew whispered in scared agreement frightened of Richard Dornman after the speech about the gun.

"Right, let's get this over with"

"Yes yes, and go" Samuel yelled.

A click on the screen from Richard created a short sound and Matthew snapped the paper up extremely scared and started to read "Mother, Father we've been kidnapped, I don't know why but you've done something. He's got a gun. Give their money back. Give up your jobs and you can have us back. They haven't hurt us yet but they won't wait long. Mother. I'm scared, come, please come.

A loud silence followed this and Richard was sat holding the phone slightly tilted, boredom all over his face as he stared, face sunken and a fly buzzing on the ceiling. He had not been bashed by the emotional words. as he slowly turned the camera at a nudge from the butler Michael and Penelope's face's widened in fear and they stared at Samuel mouthing slowly 'say something'

"If you loved us you would give up everything for us" Penelope whimpered dramatically.

``Help us" whispered Michael. This was the first time Michael had looked out of control and deeply put out. Matthew with the camera of him was focused on kicking a twig but caught up in his head wondering when mother and father would come. Penelope, however, looked happy and lively, clearly thinking this was some kind of game still, firmly looking down on Samuel and questioningly at Richard. the click came again and Michael unfroze. Penelope stretched along the floor in a huff, a cloud of dust rising above her. Samuel and Richard stomped up the stone filthy stairs without a glance at the children leaving them sad and put out like rubbish thrown into a bin.

Archie raced in a swift turn into the wide and deep gravel driveway making a loud crunch that echoed around the fields frightening a flock of crows into flight. Caroline hopped out and into a run as the car squeaked to a stop. Archie swiftly marched behind, a furious, clenched grimace upon his flushed face, eyes in slits. He whipped out his phone and saw an email from Mr Richard dornman. His pace quickened and his face reddened with rage. The door was unlocked and Caroline opened it with a flourish, expecting the children to be sitting at the kitchen table, grinning to themselves about their marvellous trick. But alas, this didn't happen. The children were well and truly gone.

Caroline bolted to the large phone that always sat in the corner of the drawing-room and perched onto an armchair clutching at the armrests, her knuckles red. She picked up the receiver quickly and swallowed down scorching sick that had flooded up her throat. She pressed down on 9, her hand shaking. She pressed the 9 again and was almost touching the third 9 when she felt a hand on her shoulder.

"What are you doing darling?" came the soft voice of her husband.

With a scared dart of the head, she said "Calling the police Archie! Our children have been kidnapped!"

"Calling the POLICE! Caroline, there will be awkward questions! Social services will get involved! We will lose our jobs!" Archie was shouting now, his face going a dark shade of magenta. "Everything I have worked for!"

Caroline bent her head.

"They are our children Archie," she said quietly to the carpet. "They will be waiting for us."

"I'd rather lose my children then lose my job."

Archie lifted Caroline up and padded to the sitting room calmly talking of another email with a video attached. Caroline was frozen, her face still with shock and horror at her husband. Her neck fell onto the back sofa and she fixed her eyes onto the screen as Archie slid his phone onto the apple pad. The video came on and Caroline's eyes widened, a sob bursting from her. Matthew's crackling voice started and the ears of Archie and Caroline pricked. As the video went on Archie's face darkened into a deep scarlet and Caroline's cheeks frosted into white, her whole body looking faint. The children were gone.

*   *   *

Michael was sitting on the cold stone floor, waiting for the Butler to come in with their midday meal. It wasn't as if he was looking forward to this, they had been positively horrible and he had a high suspicion that the food was out of date as well, as he had seen bits of green on the stiff bread only this morning. Michael looked around at Matthew, who was trying to chip a passageway through the stone with a spoon he had used at breakfast. Matthew was at least trying to help, even if it was no good, on the other hand, Penelope had spent her days locked in the room drawing pictures in the dust with a stray stick and muttering about befriending a cat, or was it a rat? Wondered Michael before he waved the thought away. No use trying to think about Penny's thoughts as they would probably be as topsy turvy as that ridiculous book he'd read last week, Alice in Wonderland.

He must talk to his siblings about a plan to escape if their parents never turned up.

However, it was Penelope who broke the silence.

"we've been here ages—my vitamin c must be as low as the number of Matt's friends, meaning none. " she cackled loudly. More nonsense thought Michael but he did give a faint sniff of amusement all the same.

"When do you think mother and father will come for us?" Matthew said, choosing to ignore the comment.

"I don't know Matthew," said Michael. "I'm bored out of my mind here and I'm still thinking about that gun."

"MICHAEL! Don't say that word!" Shrieked Penelope.

The two boys stared, their necks slightly bent in pure confusion and annoyance.

"Whatever," said Michael. "Anyway, I believe that mother and father won't come for us at all"

"Oh shush, I can't bear the thought!"

"We really should try and leave right away," said Michael, ignoring Penelope.

"But what if they do come for us and we're gone?" Inquired Matthew, his brown eyes becoming rounder.

"Ok" groaned Michael. "We never know." He rolled his eyes.

There was silence for a while until Penelope said: "what's the time?"

"Oh penny they took our watches, you silly girl"

"Oh pity I was wondering when lunch would be served"

"Penny I don't think you understand the term 'KIDNAP'."

"Michael? Michael?" Said Matthew

"Wot?"

"What if we have to stay here forever?" implored Matthew.

There was silence again.

'They'll come soon, but we can't harm the children yet"

Richard Dornman was pacing a smart, vintage room in which he and Samuel were in. Samuel was nervously perched upon a sofa, his eyes flickering around the room.

"You're going to kill them?" Came Samuel's timid voice

"We'll see, depending on how much the children mean to them. Now take them the food."

"Right away sir."

"You don't have to call me that. I'm not the ridgeways" Richard spat the last word out so some of his saliva glistened on the scruffy carpet.

"Alright," Samuel swallowed down the impulse to call him sir. "Richard"

He walked out with a tray. Lightly closing the door behind him, his white-knuckled hands curled around the sharp ridge of the door. Richard was left alone. He reached for his phone and stood still, a passive look on his face.

"Oh Richard, Oscar is missing you, come back as so as you can"

Richard sat relaxed on a large leather armchair with a crystal glass of gin and tonic held delicately between two fingers. in the other hand, a mobile phone of great quality lay also gently towards his ear.

"I promise honey, I'll be back before you know it. We can have a game of cards."

Harriet rolled her eyes and said

"Yes alright, how's your hotel, are you in London's best?"

Richard looked around at the oak wooden planks of wood that lined the floor with a rustic patterned carpet slid on top of it. At the soft armchairs, grand oak furniture and the rolling fields of the countryside outside.

"Yes it's fairly modern, I can see all the skyscrapers from the window as well." He said this cautiously, unable to know whether his lie was convincing.

"well at least your back in the city, anyway I've got to pick oscar up from school, see you Sunday"

"Goodbye, I'll be back at around four."

"Bye," said Harriet with another roll of the eyes and she put the phone down. Her eyes flickered to the dog-shaped clock and grabbed a lead and coat as their dog Rosie padded behind Harriet, the dog's claws tapping at the tiled floor. Harriet slipped into her shoes and left grabbing a hat and shoving it upon her long chestnut hair.

Samuel, on leaving the stiff and slightly awkward company of Mr Richard Dornman, headed carefully down the ruff stone stairs, a shower of brick particles spitting on to his casual checkered shirt. His hands were gripped onto a grey, plastic tray with three slop filled bowls. On coming onto level ground he smashed the tray onto half a bench that sat leaning against the peeling painted walls. His actions were much rougher away from Richard and his hatred for the children shone brightly from his eyes. At the noise of the tray, Michael and Matthew flinched while Penelope jumped in fright turning to confront Samuel in an angry tone. But at the sight of food, she jumped forward and her face turned to a disapproving look.

"About time dear butler, I'm not sure mother will be that keen to re-employ you again if you continue with this slow service."

Samuel gave Penelope an icy look and just contained his anger, said with a fake smile.

" I'm not your butler, and if you treat me like one I think I might borrow something from Mr Dornman."

"Oo is this a riddle, let's see, now who is this Mr Dornman," Penelope said under her breath, deep in thought.

"He means the gun penny"

"Yes, just shut up and listen," said Matthew in a pleading voice, his eyes flashing towards Samuel's hands.

"Right, you three will be fine as long as you do as you're told," said Samuel with a dark and shady look while Penelope gave him a sour glance of disgust. Matthew opened his mouth to talk but with a look from Michael contained himself. After a minute of silence Richard shouted.

"Hurry up Samuel"

"Oh sorry sir, just coming"

"Samuel"

"Oh yes Richard, sorry"

Samuel quickly rushed up the stairs without a glance at the children and with a slightly unnerved look on his face whipped through the door, closing it on his way out. The three children were left to slowly pad over to their bowls, they sat on a few grey, small bricks cradling their bowls and shovelling the pale porridge-like substance into their mouths in pure disgust and horror. Penelope looked fit to burst and not with excitement. Mathew placed his bowl down and stared into space, complete sadness in his face. Tears fell down his front and into his bowl. He crawled over to Michael placing his head on Michael's shoulder. Michael stared at him sadly.

"Don't worry, it will get better"

"I just want to go home" a silence fell and Penelope placed her bowl down slightly feeling she was missing out on a hug. She shuffled over and joined them. The three children were to be found sad and hungry but together still hopeful or their rescue.

Ridgeway manor was to be found grey under fog with spitting rain wettening the stone tiles of the terrace and small puddles forming on the little dips of gravel on the drive. Droplets of rain ran down the large windows and bags of water fell in heaps off the colossal, green leaves. A door was flung open and two figures sprung out large suitcases over their heads protecting them from the rain. Caroline and Archie rushed through the pouring water crunching the gravel under their feet. Caroline hung back reluctant to go but after a strict word from Archie's strong and flushed face, she rushed through into the car, a speck of anger upon her white face. Archie shoved the bags aggressively into the back of the large car and slipped hurriedly into the driving seat.

"Oh Archie, please let us come back one day for the children"

Archie gripped caroline's hand, not out of comfort, but out of fear that she would escape him, while saying,

"Yes, maybe, but we are doing this for us, let's go"

Caroline clenched her whole body and ripped her wrist from Archie's hand.

"yes, alright," she said shakily, collapsing into the seat.

The car reversed slowly and turned down the drive onto the main road where Archie picked up speed and raccd along the road vigorously splashing two elderly people on the pavement and overtaking a small mini. A determined look lay on Archie's face while carolines face fell heart stricken and blank. The couple sat in silence, pure silence. Archie glanced at two plane tickets placed carefully in the side compartment of the car with the words, destination: Egypt.

8
Who are the Ridgeway Parents?

"RIGHT: GET IN and stay here, you're not coming out until tomorrow so take your last look."

Samuel shoved the three children roughly into the cellar and down the stairs ducking under the low door frame. He was now dressed in rough jeans and a pale cream shirt, the exact opposite of what Penelope viewed as proper butlers clothes and she was just telling him so as she trotted down. Matthew and Michael were looking grim while Samuel was looking murderous as he so often did near the ridgeway children.

That morning, Samuel had woken up in his own house, the rough wooden barn with small windows. He had kissed his children good morning and told luke what he was to do for the day. With a grateful smile at his eldest son, a thought of how old he was getting and the prospect of how he would cope without Luke, he slowly shoved over to the door. He grabbed at an umbrella, thoughts of his wife returning to him and once wiping this sad thought away he had left the house and been picked up by

Richard. The awkward silence had filled the car once again. Once there, Samuel remembered in great disappointment that he was not done with these children and their spoilt, bratty manner still filled his day. As his mind crawled back to the present penelope asked

"may I ask when my lunch will be served because I like to plan my day and I would not like lunch to get in the way"

"Your lunch will be served," he said sarcastically

"When I feel like it, you might not get it at all."

"Well that wasn't very helpful but" she drowned off and entered into the corner. Penelope seemed to still not understand the meaning of kidnap, although she had become more motherly to Matthew which you could see as a positive. Matthew also slumped down into the dust which had somehow reformed in the five minutes that the children had been in the loo. Michael however halted and stayed on the last step with a slightly rebellious look on his face. Samuel, not knowing this walked back up the stairs once again ignoring any remarks made by the children. Michael swiftly and quietly followed Samuel up the stairs and as Samuel closed the door and strolled away Michael carefully slipped his foot creating a gap and stopping the shutting of the door. Although a searing pain had just entered his ankles, the plan had worked.

An argument had started between Matthew and Penelope about who lost the stick they both used for drawing in the dust. Matthew was standing up yelling at Penelope while she sat down, her legs wide staring at the floor while talking annoyingly about where she put the stick last time. Michael with a roll of the eyes shouting over to them both "you two be quiet and come here, lets see what they have been saying."

"But how?"

"Yes if you hadn't noticed we don't have extendable ears" Said penelope with an all-knowing look

"what, what an earth are to talking about?," Matthew said confused

"Oh lord Matthew, harry potter!" she said like she was explaining what one plus one equalled.

"Argh, Fred and George use these in the order of the Phoenix," she said loudly.

"I'm surprised she can read!" Matthew muttered in an undertone.

"How rude, and i didnt read, I watched the films," she said, like suddenly having won the argument. An angry retort had sizzled up Matthew's throat but Michael spoke out first.

"Just ignore her," he said while starting up on telling them his plan.

"You see I stopped the door."

"Oh, that's why you followed the butler," said Matthew

"Wait, I'm confused, what?" Said penelope

Michael went on and explained slowly how he followed the butler while grabbing Matthews two shoulders and moving him to the door.

"Well, you could have told me all that, you know I can't read minds."

Both Michael and Matthew sighed deeply and rolled their eyes. The three children then shuffled out of the door and looked both ways. They crept carefully on tiptoes across the red, diamond shaped and tiled corridor, then heard faint voices from the room ahead.

"Right, let's listen," Michael whispered, barely opening his mouth.

Not knowing of the children's plan, Richard once again lay relaxed on an armchair, a drink in hand, unfocused and talking automatically to Samuel, who was crouched down lighting a fire while quietly behind him just creeping their eyes round the door stood Penelope, Michael and Matthew their ears pricked and listening carefully.

"I still can't believe he tricked you!" started up Samuel trying hard to break the silence

"I know! And he's been doing it for decades," answered Richard in a sneer.

"I always knew he was quite fishy," said Samuel, a suspicious look on his face.

Penelope whispered to Michael from out the door "He smelt of peppermint to me!"

This was ignored by Michael who crouched a little nearer pressing his ear closer to the white and slightly cold door while muttering something about this being very important and that she would never take anything seriously. Penelope began to argue in answer to this but was held up by a finger being put to her lips by Matthew.

"Any way Samuel, go and check the tea will you, I like mine without milk," said Richard in a strong and slightly bored voice

"Oh yes, I'll go now" Samuel pushed himself up onto his two thin and quite fragile legs and started to open the door. In a roar of movement and whispers, the three children shuffled to the cellar in a panic. Phrases like 'hurry up' and 'move' echoed in the corridor thankfully not heard by Samuel, and Penelope, Michael and Matthew shoved themselves in carefully, closing the door while staring at each other in fear. The same thought of 'that was close' entering their minds.

While creeping down the rough and worn stairs the children began to Whisper, their eye brows furrowed about all that they had just heard. Chatter dispersed between them on the job of their parents and how they couldn't have known. A silence occurred for a split second before Michael started

"Do you know what this means,"

"What that fathers smuggling fish,"

Said Penelope who had somewhat been in her own world for the last 5 minutes and was still puzzled by the conversation between Richard and Samuel. Michael and matthew fell silent for a minute in pure annoyance before michael started up,

"So they said something was always fishy about our parents and that they cheated Richard out of money, but how," Penelope gave an indignant cry "what, How DARE they say father smelt!"

"Argh, Penny just listen to Michael, you don't always have to talk."

"Actually, talking is the best way to communicate ideas so I see it as pretty darn helpful,"

This comment was passed off and as Michael and Matthew started to slump down onto a few less pointy boxes, Penelope sighed and gave a short dissatisfied sound at being ignored. However she did finally kneel down her long blonde hair flopping down with her. Michael leaned towards her.

"Anyway, Our parents have stolen money from that man Richard and now he has kidnapped us, how do you think they did it though?, "

"Well we know,, they shoved into a car and left, don't you remember?" called Penelope.

"No, I mean how did they steal money from Richard."

"Maybe it's their job. You know the house selling" Matthew wondered aloud.

"Or," Penelope said, like her idea was a much more likely story.

"That can of baked beans father brought home a few nights back, well what if they were actually from that man, Ronald,"

"Richard," popped in Michael.

"No Michael, I'm Penelope, you really are losing your marbles today."

"No I mean, the man you just called Ronald is actually called Richard." said Michael, his teeth clenched in annoyance.

"Michael you're interrupting, anyway, that's why, he was so angry and that's why he kidnapped us. it's the only possible answer." Penelope finished with an almost questioning look like she wanted the boys to try and prove her wrong.

With a look of disgust and slight anger from Matthew he said

"Firstly why would a can of baked beans cost £1.5 million and secondly,"

"Just drop it, she's bonkers." said Michael.

"Alright be like that, just know that when we find out I was right the 'words I told you so' shall be coming out of my mouth several times."

"Ok, just let me and Matthew think for a while," said Michael and he turned to Matthew and started to talk sharply and fast About all subjects around their parents and escaping the dark and dank cellar. Penelope heaved, her arms crossed still looking straight at Michael and Matthew but after a while perched on one of the stairs playing with an imaginary teddy.

Planes lifted off the ground, soaring up, up to far off countries. Crowds of people, endlessly waiting, shuffling into shops, drifting up and down escalators. Caroline and Archie, however, were found strolling into the first class lounge. Plucking finger sandwiches from white, gleaming plates. they perched, tensely waiting, on violently green circular chairs. The room was empty, the slight sound of clattering cutlery magnified in the silence. While Archie automatically pulled out his phone to look at the news, Caroline sat staring straight ahead, her eyes unfocused, a worried and slightly faint look upon her face.

After half an hour with hardly any movement apart from the swipe of Archie's finger on his phone. he gave a quick glance around the room, he swiftly heaved the two lilac suitcases across the floor and stood up, heading to the other side of the modern, simplistic room towards a white door.

"Right dear, we are off. The plane is leaving in 15."

"yes, alright" Caroline gulped in a soft whimpering voice. The couple left, leaving the white door to swing depressingly and the stewards to stand, a little abashed.

"Oh Caroline, do be quick, if we miss this plane."

" yes, yes"

Archie was striding long and loud steps down an infinite corridor with large windows filling the extensive walls and tiny wheels of suitcases rolling beside his feet. Caroline was drifting along like a pale ghost, feelings sucked from her body. She was tired of this constant 'Simon says', she wanted her own life. She wanted her children back but was too afraid to do it.

9
Still in the Cellar

WHILE CAROLINE AND Archie sat still and quiet on a plane, the children remained bad tempered and annoyed in the rough and dark cellar.

"We need a plan to find out more information" put in Michael, breaking the quietness sharply, as per usual in these regular silences.

"How can we do it though?" questioned Matthew, biting his lip.

"We could try what we did yesterday and sneak up behind the door to listen in at their conversation?"

"Yes, fine let us try that then"

"Or," muttered Penelope, not taking her eyes off the spot where she was picking the peeling wallpaper, "we could see if he has anything in his pockets that could help us when he brings down dinner."

The other two stared at her, partly because they had forgotten she was there and partly because of this simply good idea.

"Penny that's the best idea you've had in weeks!" Stuttered Michael.

"Well, it did seem as if a light bulb went off in my head." she replied matter of factly.

"Are we ready? Michael stand behind the door and Penny and I will be in this corner." said Matthew, keen to be the subject of the conversation again.

As Michael nodded, a slight shriek from Penelope told them that the Butler was on his way.

Samuel Wilkinson came plodding down the stairs in the familiar style that occurred every day, his large feet clumping at a steady beat onto the stone. A heavily bored look hung onto his face and he placed the tray automatically onto the same old box while muttering something about dinner. This movement however unabled Michael to move ahead of Samuel and an annoyed expression filled his cheeks. Penelope, having unusually not made a remark to the butler, gave a smart little grin and whipped her hand overdramatically into the butler's pocket. She then heaved out a small mobile phone before shaking it wildly over Samuels head towards Michael and Matthew. A smug look arose as she slapped it down onto her hand and slipped it into her left pocket while giving a large and obvious wink to Matthew and Michael.

Once the whole movement had halted and Samuel walked stiffly back up the stairs oblivious to all that had happened, the children began to chatter about what had just happened.

"I've got his phone" remarked Penelope, holding up the device with a flourish.

"OK, go over here," put in Michael, stabbing at the phone with a long finger, "open messages from Richard"

"Alright, keep your encyclopedias inside your pockets" said Penelope. clearly struggling to find the messages button.

Michael snatched the phone from her "I'll read it out."

"Oh fine." she muttered under her breath "I *was* the one who got the actual phone but of course YOU have to do everything."

"That's because you're as dumb as a cow" whispered Matthew with a snigger. He very rarely thought up a good joke on the spot and he was feeling rather smug.

"Shut up Mat-"

"Shush you two." Michael cleared his throat.

"Samuel."

"That must be the name of the butler! How did we never know?" whispered Matthew in hushed tones.

"Remember why we are kidnapping those wicked children" went on Michael.

"Remember how Mr and Mrs Ridgeway cheated me and charged me 1.5 million for an old, run down shack. Remember how rude and disrespectful that family has been to you. They are bad people. Criminals. We need to teach them a lesson. It's only a matter of time." Michael paused. Then continued, in a shaking voice,

"So now we know. Our parents are criminals."

Everyone looked at the floor, not wanting to speak first, not wanting to say the dreaded truth.

Then Penelope broke the silence in her matter of fact tone,

"I wish we didn't to be honest"

"Yes i know but they still love us and i'm sure they'll come back for us."

"Well said Matt. Always keep a positive attitude—at least that's what my toy koala always said!"

"Alright Penny…"

$$* \qquad * \qquad *$$

Oh I wish mother and father would hurry up and rescue us." Said Penelope, speaking her unwanted mind—as usual.

"Oh shut up Pen" Matthew said, losing his temper.

"Ok you two, calm down. Penelope, don't annoy everyone please."

"You weren't like that when Matt called me a cow!"

"Actually, it was an idotic cow!" Matthew grinned mischievously.

"Oh shu-" But mid sentence Michael pulled Penelope over to the door and beckoned Matthew over. They pushed their ears to the cold stone door, listening hard.

"Well," The cold, strong voice of Mr Richard Dornman spoke up.

"The parents are obviously not going to show up, they have left for egypt. We might as well dispose of the little brats."

"Wow. I thought their parents cared for them.

"The voice of Samuel carried through the door, colder still than the children had ever heard him speak.

"But of course nothing is as important to them as their money and career."

"I did tell you they were heartless and cold, in that phone call, do you remember?"

"Yes I remember. We'd better dispose of them quickly before they tell anyone about their little holiday."

"Sounds like a plan. See you tomorrow night at 2am."

The sound of padding footsteps slowly softened as the two men strolled away, their heads bending in a smart nod. Matthew slumped down onto the dirty floor, his eyes unfocused, breathing hard. He could not believe this. It wasn't true! But something in the back of his head was telling him that his father and mother had really left them for good.

10
Overflowing Bins

WELL I'M GLAD." Penelope said, as her brothers sat on the floor, despair washing over them like icy water. They were sat once more on the same boxes that had certainly become too familiar for the children's liking. All three had been fed up with this celler for weeks. The carpets of dust, the rotten old boxes, the gloop that was fed to them. It had to go.

As this comment was made, Michael and Matthew's hands were deep into their heads depressed, terrorfied and most of all angry. Michael said between his fingers.

"Why?, why would you be glad?"

"Well the bins have been overflowing for days—it's high time they dispose of the rubbish." she said matter of factly, her sharp voice cutting into the miserable air.

"No Penelope. They're going to dispose of us." Matthew gulped. "They're going to kill us."

"Wait." Michael was staring hard at his sister. "How do *you* know that the bins are overflowing? There are no windows underground." He bashed the wall and immediately regretted it—his hand was all dirty now.

"Oh there's a lovely view of the garden from the window in the bathroom they take me to. Do you boys have a window in your bathroom? I even sometimes take a breath of the fresh air!"

The atmosphere had changed, hope radiated from michael and matthew and they leant forwards eager to know more.

"Penny, do you know what this means?"

"Well it sure as well means that we can pop out for a game of croquet anytime soon—so don't look so glum Matt. Oh but one of the adults won't be able to play. Ah, no matter, they can be umpire.

"Oh no! One of the people who is trying to kill us will be *so* upset!" Matthew said sarcastically.

"Don't worry!" Penelope said, genuinely concerned. "We'll make a tournament of it!"

A knock on the door interrupted Matthew's next spiteful comment before it was even out of his mouth. The Butler entered the room, halting momentarily with a suspicious look towards their smiling faces. He brushed this off and stepped down.

"It's time for you to go to the loo now."

Michael opened his mouth to reply but Penelope got there first.

"Oh don't worry, we don't need to go, Michael was just saying."

Samuel, again, cast a suspicious eye over Michael and Matthew's shocked faces before he turned, muttering,

"alright" and slammed the door behind him. There was a long and still silence in the humid air. Clouds of dust formed around them as michael and matthew slowly tilted their heads in anger towards penny

71

"Penny!"

"What? just being helpful."

"Penny!"

"Who should tell her?"

"I'll take the honor, You see, now that our parents are in Egypt we know they're not coming to get us so we need to find a way to escape! And then you mentioned this window that we can get through, so that's how we escape, Penelope, by using the window in your loo."

"I prefer to call it a lavatory but, go on."

"That's it, We've told you everything Penny. Now, we need to think of a plan to get me and you, Michael into Penny's Loo."

"How do we do it without being caught?"

"Don't worry, I've got a plan!"

"Are you sure that will work?—your plans are normally disastrous, and you ARE eight."

"OH Michael have some faith."

After rehearsing over and over all night with his siblings, by the next morning, Michael felt he and the others were ready.

"Right, the plan is in action—we all know what to do."

"Ok, the Butler should be coming to get us about now, he normally comes at this sort of time."

The children moved automatically to the door. There was only one suitable crack to peek through, and, surprise surprise, Penelope got there first.

"Right Penny you need to tell us when the Butler's coming."

"Alright." Penelope whispered back, pleased to have some authority over her brothers.

The boys started muttering about the plan when Penelope whispered loudly,

"He's coming!"

Samuel burst through the door. It seemed that he always wanted to catch the children doing something they shouldn't as he threw open the door so suddenly.

"Right, Penny, you come with me, boys you know where your loo is, your sister, however is a bit 'unique' in her head so I'm taking her. And don't try anything, I'm watching, always watching."

The boys headed out to their loo, whispering about getting ready for Penelope's signal and why the plan was placed on her hands, not Michaels, for instance. They unconsciously tiptoed across the cold tiles of the pathway, Matthew grasing his hand on the slightly bubbly white walls while craning their to spy on where Richard was off too. A huge shadow lay sat on a leather armchair letting the boys know they were good to go. A frantic shuffling followed and the boys were in place for the plan. Whispers of good luck ran from their mouths and they froze ready for action

Back in the cellar, Penelope was having a lovely time, as she purposely dropped her button on the floor.

"Oops! Would you pick that up for me Butler?"

"I'm NOT your Butler anymore," Samuel said. Tight lipped.

"You do realise that, don't you? Even so, I'll pick it up for you." As Samuel picked up the button Penelope purposely flicked another one onto the floor, a cheeky grin forming on her face.

"Oh no oh no, I really do think I'm losing my marbles today, or should I say buttons! Could you pick that up for me too?" Penelope sighed and yelled with laughter while Samuel's face was left looking murderous.

"Why can't you?" Samuel said stiffly.

"Oh, I have rather have a stiff back if you must know. Hurry up now."

Samuel rolled his eyes as he bent down for the second time. Then he took hold of Penelope's shoulders and sterered her forcefully towards her bathroom. Where he shoved her in, oblivious to the shadow of two boys behind the door, and muttered for her to be quick.

"Oh I can't wait for two aclock," siad Samuel with a menacing grimace as he swiftly clumped back to the sitting room, the thought of waiting for Penelope to finish leaving his mind.

Penelope, having firmly shut the door and just about to walk over to the loo, stopped sharply and stared at the other two standing triumphantly by the sink. The bathroom was fully tiled in green and Michael stood excited with his hands together, an appraisal grin on his face while Matthew sat down onto the loo seat with a similar look.

"Dear lord, why all the trouble just so you can use my bathroom, I mean I know it's nice but use your own!"

"Oh penn…"

"Just ignore, right well done, the hard part's over, now let's get out of here."

"WHAT I NEED THE LOO!" Penelope was shouting now. "And i'd like some privacy"

"Oh you can hold it."

"A LADY SHOULD NEVER HOLD HER WATER!"

"Shut up you two, right Matt, you go over first."

"Mind you don't hurt yourself!" Penelope squealed, suddenly more motherly than she'd ever been in her life.

"Whatever." Matthew said dismissively.

Onc by one, they all climbed onto the roof, down a helpful willow tree and onto the overflowing bins that Penelope had so

74

remembered. They all jumped down onto the lawn with an exhausted look upon their faces and crossed the busy road taking a half jog just before a blue car raced past, Michael pulling each of them by the arms, terrorfied at being chased after.

They headed straight for the fields which lay ahead and stepped off the hot, black tarmac and onto the pages of long waving grass that stood before them. No one looked back. Michaels head swung back and forth, his brain working hard to decide the way and lead the small group towards the east. Michael was for once scared. His mind having been filled to the brim and working non stop to escape and to find out who their parents truly were, never spent one moment imagining what they were to do if they actually ended up escaping. Now, however, his mind was being piled heavily with plans and possible ideas while thoughts of what could happen to them now they were all alone rushed frantically through his brain. While still leading a steady pace, he took many deep breaths to try and clear his mind. Matthew was feeling many of the same feelings as well but was also so overwhelmed that he was left almost empty, just his muscles working with the beat of his breath.

The children ran on, silhouettes in the morning sunlight. They had fallen into a silence following the stress and excitement of several hours before. Finding themselves opening onto a large rolling field filled with large patterned ruts and dried, dark brown mud, the three children started into a run, led by Michael. Twice Matthew got a stitch, unable to keep up with his two siblings, but Michael heaved him up, egging him to speed on, to not get caught. After about half an hour, however, Matthew finally snapped.

"I give UP." he moaned, scuffing his feet through the dirt. "I'm tired of running. I want to go home." and with that he sat down on the ground with a bump as Michael and Penelope exchanged worried glances.

"Well Matthew," said Michael, squatting down onto the floor beside him, "I'm sure we could go home."

"You mean it?"

"Well not forever, but maybe to gather some things like clothes."

"And teddies!"

"Yes Pen and teddies."

"But I want to live with mother and father just like it was before all this trouble happened."

"Matt," Soothed Michael, glaring at Penelope, who was being no help at all, "we are not going home because mother and father have gone, life can't carry on like it always was."

"And Matthew" Penelope buttered in, finally taking the hint from Michael's continuous glares, "Some people just need to find a new family, start again. Some people just weren't started off on the right footing.

Thoughts of 'we'll go with that' flooded Michael's brain, but he tactfully kept silent. Michael had never been tactful before. It was a nice feeling, and Michael somehow, felt different to his old self.

The three children wandered into a soft silence, Michael and Penelope were worn out and didn't want to increase the annoyance of Matthew. With thoughts of why we didnt have lunch before they left in Penelope's head and thousands of memories and ideas on where to go next from Michael, the small group headed on slowly slipping into a steady walk.

"I forgot, we have the butlers phone, let's use the map," shrieked Michael with a pointed finger in the air.

"Oh good, I didn't feel like following your directions. We might have ended up in France" Penelope said, giving a little laugh. She was, however, disappointed at the silence from Matthew. He was looking more solemn and miserable as the long trek wore on.

Michael whipped out Samuel's phone and started to study the flickering screen swiping before his eyes.

Hours past and three shadows strolled past a few signs and into a small village which glowed as yellow fiery lights flickered on in the square windows of houses. Lunchtimes bright shine had flown into dusk and the sun began to lower creating a musty lense upon the houses and roads around them. They strolled onto the slick, grey pavement and faced towards a pair of golden plated gates that hung smartly before a winding driveway that led to the familiar navy door and pale stoned terrace, Their eyes flickering to the slab of wood that read ridgeway manor.

"Right here we are, now Matthew we are not staying. Let's whip our stuff and head off" Michael said in a business like manner.

"Well I quite agree and let us remember that our parents have left for somewhere abroad. They've left us."

"Alright," Matthew said timidly.

"Hang on a second" Penelope spoke clearly into the silent surroundings.

"We can't travel in this light, we shall have to stay a night." Michael began to stutter his disapproval at this but Penelope went on about how it was the only way and darkness would not help their travels,

"Well alright, let's get in, have a quick supper and pack *before* we go to sleep. We shall leave sharp in the morning" settled Michael continuing his military voice and slightly disappointed he didn't have paper to write a check list. With a roll of the eyes from Penelope, the children continued to stride towards the house, two slightly repulsed looks upon the twin's faces. Matthew quickened his pace, however, and faintly smiled as he looked around the flower beds and hedges that surrounded the terrace. He so wanted to stay, to live life like before but that was simply not an option and Matthew would have to accept it. Michael swiftly snatched sharply at the spare keys placed carefully on the door arch before shoving it into the keyhole and opening the door. His face showed guilt and slight disgust as he said.

"Argh, when I think of this place, I just remember what kind of people we were. I vow to change from that spoiled old self."

"Ditto," called Penelope starting to enjoy this new phrase.

They shuffled in, Matthew flicking the switch and closed the door to find the same old smell and look of the grand kitchen. Quick as a wink, Michael scurried to the fridge, grabbed three, old looking apples, a few of Caroline's favourite energy bars and a packet of biscuits.

"Right, here we go, supper!"

"Great," Penelope said, her smile falling slowly as she stared at the greying apples and bars with the words 'Keep Healthy' written in bold. This was certainly not her ideal dinner, and found herself thinking of the old gloop given by the butler in the cellar almost longingly. Matthew's face was expressionless and he grabbed a bar and an apple before plodding upstairs, not a word uttering from his mouth. Michael, looking slightly confused and worried pulled his whole body back together in a sharp nod and shoved on after matthew, through the corridor and up the stairs maintaining the controlling shout,

"Hurry! Get packing and then get straight into bed!"

"Ok, ok!" muttered Penelope, rolling her eyes while dropping an apple thrown down by michael. She picked it up, disgustedly and squirmed as another bruise was planted into the tinged red fruit before dragging her legs up the stairs.

10 minutes later, each child was to be found in their own large bedroom, packing madly. Matthew was tearing things off the wall, sniffing louding, stuffing everything into his train patterned suitcase. Penelope was trying to shove all her colossal teddies into her rainbow suitcase. Alas, the big, brown bear was to be left behind. She did, however, fit in several long sleeved shirts of all colours and a pair of trousers or two. By the time her bag was zipped shut, she collapsed huffing and puffing at all the work. Michael was carefully folding all his clothes that he would need and putting some notebooks and pens into the smaller section of his black briefcase. He took no toys, as he believed they held 'too much emotional attachment'.

Finished with his packing now, Michael rounded the corner that led to Penelope's room and told her swiftly to get into bed, still staring at his eyes from the bedroom sign, he so dearlyn loathed. Penelope, huffly obliged but muttered

"I thought, supper was in the calendar for about now but it seems not. No matter, no matter,"

"You can have your bar in bed," Michael said coldly before padding off to Matthew's room, intending to do the same, but found the room deserted. Michael did not have to wonder where Matthew was. He walked towards the huge master bedroom and found Matthew sitting on the huge bed and sniffing into Caroline's best silk hankie. He put his arm around his younger brother's shaking shoulders and muttered about getting a good night's sleep. Michael guided Matthew out of his parents room and into Matthew's own, closing the door carefully. With a sag of the mattress, the boys plopped onto the bed and Michael tucked Matthew between the train sheets, where he lay, blissfully warm. He then kissed his sibling on the forehead and left the room, shutting the door behind him and turning on the landing light—he knew Matthew had never liked the dark.

11
Saying Goodbye

THE SUN WAS just peeping its head over large black hills far beyond when Michael flapped his curtains open, taking in the last time his eyes would meet this view. Almost counting on the other two to still be lounging in bed, he once again found one of them missing. This time, however, Matthew was to be found face down onto his pillow, his mouth open wide, while Penelope was nowhere to be seen. This mystery was slowly answered as Michael hopped down the curving stairs, through a large entrance room and into the same old kitchen to find Penelope the other side of the counter, a pan in her hand. As this was the first time Michael had seen Penelope doing any kind of house work, especially with a smile sketched upon her face, he was somewhat dumbfounded and froze in surprise for a manner of seconds. Penelope Rose Ridgeway was standing tall next to the hob, with a pan of scrambled egg in one hand and bacon sizzling upon another job. She was once again slightly nodding her head and humming quietly. Furthermore as Michael's eyes fell on the old, wooden slab in the middle of the room, he saw a fully laid table up to the standards of their old cook (Michael had never bothered to learn her name) and a pile of pancakes at the center of it, a drizzle of lemon draped on top.

"Penelope, what is this, you've made us breakfast!" he said, fully bemused and slightly scared, a feeling he could never have predicted.

"Oh Michael, you're down. Well, i thought that i should start taking up the role of a mother, i mean a normal one. so, here we are, pancakes and all."

"Um this is wonderful but are you sure you know how to cook all these things, i mean pancakes."

"Michael, I shall ignore the rudeness in that sentence but dont think I approve of it, and i just looked in this big book. It took me an age to find. I mean what on earth is a glossary?"

Michael, practically unable to say anything, just turned and jumped over excitedly back towards Matthew's room, a yell erupting from his mouth.

"Matthew, come down here, Penelope's made breakfast!"

And the next half hour was spent ravenously feasting upon Penelope's fine work, she had never got so much praise before and she rather liked it.

"Maybe I should become a cook." both boys went silent. Clearly they felt maybe her talents were not quite up to that standard.

While the thought of leaving had not entered their minds once with this huge surprise, as the scratching knives and forks came to an abrupt stop and the last few crumbs were scrubbed off with a finger, that dreadful feeling returned to Matthew. Penelope and Michael sensed this and knew what they must do. With a quick glance at each other, they said together.

"Matthew it will be fine, just look at it this way, we can start a new life, a new adventure."

"Yes, it's like getting a new teddy, you don't quite know if you will like it as much as the one before but it's fun and exciting and you always do." Sung Penelope like this settled the matter and would make Matthew feel much better.

"Yes, just like that." said Michael, as confused as he always was when his sister said something like this. While Michael went on with a few kind words, Penelope nodded her head vigorously like this would tempt Matthew into feeling excited. The grand entrance room lay clean with an ever so thin layer of dust creeping among the surfaces of the shiny, oak tables and golden plated picture frames. A large circular table lay smartly in the middle of the room and the children shuffled in reasonably fastly, wanting to get on. A slow shuffle came from Matthew, however and his eyes twitched from spot to spot, taking in the whole room, he was finally dragged to the door by penelope and they rambled through leaving the grounds of their familiar stately home empty. And empty it would be for several years to come.

Michael banged the door shut as they all left their once homely manor. Matthew shook his head slightly as he tried to not think about whether this was the last time he would see the great navy blue door swing closed.

Penelope hoisted her rainbow backpack higher up her back, impatient to leave. This place had too many muddled memories. Grabbing Matthew's hand because she knew he was apprehensive to leave, she strode onto the gravel driveway whilst telling Michael in a manner rather like his own, to get a move on otherwise we'll never get there!

They all hurried out of the gates, at a loss to decide where to go. Finally, Michael spoke up,

"I think i know where we should go…"

"Where?"

"Well you know where mother's best friend Margret worked?" He glanced at his sibling's blank faces and sighed. "Didn't you listen, I mean I do have an exceptional hearing range so i am not surprised and well, anyway, she worked at a place—i can't remember the exact term, but it helped children like us," he squeezed Matthew's hand.

"Find a new family."

Matthew gulped, swallowing his growing sob. He didn't like this new idea of starting afresh and was rather worried about it. What if no one wanted them? What if they were split up? What if a horrible person took charge of them? He did not voice his feelings to the others, thinking that they would laugh outwardly at his fears, crushing his hopes of having supporting siblings.

"So where *is* this place then Michael?" Penelope inquired.

"Ummm, I think it's in the next village." Michael's face suddenly lit up. "Wait! I have an idea! How about we cycle there! It'll be much quicker mind you."

Five minutes later and the children were speeding out of the driveway, on top of the range bikes, racing through the country lanes towards the next village, Cimberly. It was a large village, and had all the necessary requirements, lots of small shops including a supermarket, a tiny park and best of all, many grand houses. Yes, Michael still liked a large house. He came to a stop, thinking of doing a cool skid like in the films but thought 'best not', as he wouldn't want to hurt himself now. Penelope and Matthew followed suit and much to the annoyance of Michael, Penelope managed the cool looking skid without even realising it.

"Now I'm sure it was this street, but which door."

"Oh Michael, for once in your life use your eyes instead of thinking every little equation and scenario in your head. It says orphanage," penelope called tantalisingly while pointing towards a plank of wood among a white, metal fence.

"I'm guessing you know what an orphanage is then,"

"Well yes of course, really, first you don't look and now you don't listen,"

Puzzled looks from Michael and Matthew followed these words and Penelope, greatly enjoying the fact that she knew something the other two didn't, started up smugly.

"An orphanage is a place where they take in children like us, the tutor said so in an English lesson, remember about the play 'Annie'," at these words Michael clapped a hand to his mouth, he had never forgotten one thing from his lessons and now, well at least Penelope remembered.

"Yes your right Penn, let's go,"Michael called keen to take back the authority.

They walked towards a faded white door holding a large gold 9 in the centre. On one side of the door a letterbox was hanging off on one hinge, on the other a dying pot plant lay sad upon a wooden shelf. It was not a pleasant sight and made the children worry about what it would hold inside. Michael stopped confidently up the short stairs, not wanting to show Matthew that he was in any doubt. He raised his long finger to the large doorbell and pressed down hard. Nothing happened. He did it again. There was no ringing sound, no clattering run from inside. He tried twice more but, again, with no effect. Sighing, he pushed his hand into a fist and knocked sharply on the black, peeling door.

12
Number 9, Cimberly

THE DOOR OPENED. A plump woman, dressed in overalls emerged, a smile stretched across her face. She had mousy hair which matched her hazel eyes and had a streak of brown on one rosy cheek—Michael assumed it was chocolate sponge batter.

"Hello dears!" She said in a pleasant voice. "What can i do for you?"

"Umm we were wondering if we could talk to Margaret" said Michael, his confident walk and voice having suddenly vanished.

"In PRIVATE." butted in Penelope, noticing the children lurking round the door, their ears pricked.

"Alright, you better come in, but we're quite busy at the moment, by the way I'm, Im, Im Mrs carmichael but you can call me poppy" she said almost shouting over the wailes and shouts from the background before staring reproachfully at the children's bags and Matthew's tear stained face.

"It will only be quick," said Michael, his natural and strong voice returning. The plump woman waved an arm inside and the children followed. They crept into a white washed corridor with a crooked little shoe rack hung on one side, piles of shoes, coats and all sorts among it. The children, whose eyes had been peeping round the door came into view and it was a comforting thought to see that they were well clothed and looked rather churpy. Penelope's face however fell at the thought that she had just walked into having several more siblings which was not to her taste. A roll of stairs flooded up the other side to find 5 more children sitting on top of the soft, grey carpet. All eyes were on the children. Matthew felt scared and the new feeling of wanting to shrink into your own shell came.

They were ushered into a room with squishy sofas and walls full of a dark green. Flowery lamps dotted the corners, creating a cosy light around the room. This brought a smile onto Penelope's faces as she loved patterns and colour. Michaels face slightly dropped however and he thought

"Would have preferred a planer room but this will have to do." The plump woman told them all to 'have a seat' and bustled off, closing the door behind her. Matthew's eyes once again flashed around the room and took in the collection of pictures. They all had different cats on. Penelope noticed this as well and settled for saying,

"Oh, she's a cat woman, well could have been worse, at least it's not snakes. Although I will not be sleeping here, all the eyes would make me go crazy."

Michael sized Matthew close to him and they half hugged each other on the sofa, whilst Penelope sat close to a lamp, her eyes tracing the flowery pattern before moving up to a large picture of a gigantic ginger tom, whose nose was squashed and underneath inscripted 'crookshanks'.

"Well at least she is a Harry Potter fan." Penelope whispered to Michael, eyeing the picture.

"Well whatever she is she's not too punctual, it's been eight minutes!" Exclaimed Michael checking his watch.

"Lord, you must be disappointed."

"Well yes, I was, we may have to change some rules here, i don't want another child coming in and thinking the exact same."

The door opened swiftly, to reveal a tall, thin woman, with slightly ginger hair and a subtle fringe. The children stared at her, overcome by fond memories of her and their mother taking tea together whilst the children had always said 'good day'.

"Hello children," Margaret looked at the children for a moment, then did a double take. "Wait, I know you, the Ridgeway's! Well why on earth are you here?" she said with a kind but questioning smile.

"Um, you see it's quite a long story." Michael said awkwardly.

"Well I'm here to listen, last time I saw you was a few months back with your mum, Caroline." she said as she sat down beside Penelope. A tear dropped down Matthew's face.

"Oh dear, are you alright?" Margaret said, her face scrunched up in sympathy

"He's fine, you'll understand when we tell you the whole story."

"Ok, I'm ready" she said, still with a sweet motherly voice. So while Penelope started up with another tune under her breath and Matthew sat silently still a little sad, Michael went through all that had happened since the very time of kidnap by Mr Richard Dornman and Samuel to the grand escape conjured up by

Penelope. Margaret's mouth opened in horror as Michael went through what their parents did and how they fled the country. She then jumped up to hug Matthew as she heard the treatment that the children were given in the cellar. Michael ended with how they got to the orphanage and when the final silence came he collapsed, his brain, for the first time, tired, into the red chair. Margaret was frozen, a constant sympathetic look on her face. Penelope however looked as if she had woken up from a trance as she changed from hovering in a cloudy dance to a strong, thin face. She obviously wanted to look like she was very much listening and taking everything extremely seriously.

"Oh dears, well I never knew such a story. Anyway, here's what we're going to do. You will have a bed in this orphanage for as long as you may need it and we can try and find you a family." Margaret said, smiling towards the children and standing up wiping some dust off her apron.

"Yes, that's just what we thought you could do. Thank you so much."

"Not at all, come with me, I've got two rooms next to each other, then I can move dear Charlie down a floor and you can all be together."

"Thank you Margaret, sounds as good as a butterfly on fire."

"Oo, a good simile Penny."

"Why thank you Michael, we should always be practising our English."

*　　　*　　　*

Margaret led the way up the carpeted stairs still speaking about all the children who lived here. The kids who had been hanging around when the Ridgeway's had arrived were in the cantine, according to Margaret, which pleased Matthew immensely—he didn't want to be stared at.

Michael, Matthew and Penelope wandered behind Margaret across the crinkled wooden floor as she swiftly chatted a tour of the orphanage.

"So, back there was the cantine, and these are all rooms for children. It's the summer holidays so no school at the moment but we will find you one when it comes to that."

"Alright," said Matthew, speaking for the first time in quite a while, he was yet to get used to the orphanage. In comparison to this, however, Penelope was popping off with questions walking haphazardly and almost toppling over a little table while gabbling random sentences clearly not sensing the tone of the time. Margaret stopped and turned before three doors

"Here we are, come in."

The first room they entered was to be Matthew's and was a bright baby blue with a long string of bunting running through the centre. He had a small, wooden bed with two little bedside tables. It was certainly comfortable and Matthew's expression lightened, just a touch.

The next room was named Michael's and it was bright green. Though his eyes winced at the colour on the walls he said cheerfully,

"I could get used to this"

Penelope's room was a bubblegum lilac but sadly not much more of the room was to be seen as Penelope rushed in gabbling about needing the loo dreadfully and closed the door squealing

"I should like some privacy"

Their first meal of the day arrived in the form of lunch and the three children shuffled in awkwardly and sat on a white, metal table that tilted one way looking as if one's food wouldn't stay on. Baked beans, cheese and toast was shuffled onto the table by a thin, spindly woman who Penelope described as 'fork like'. They dove into the food which Michael and Matthew thought was in their words 'pretty darn good'.

Apart from the chilling and silent stares the other children had given them, the meal went rather well. Penelope said nothing for a while which was extremely unusual but as expected finally remarked,

"Yes, yes, pretty good. The toast could be toasted about 17 seconds more for my liking and I prefer a less hot bean but, yes, understandable choices." Before clearly adding to Matthew and Michael,

"Yes, 8 and a half from me,"

"At least we know Penelope hasn't changed" whispered Michael constantly trying to make Matthew feel better. He chuckled weakly but it was better than nothing.

The rest of the day pleasantly passed, Penelope gave the whole orphanage a jolly good search while Michael started to chit chat with the other orphans. This didn't go too well as the children were not too interested in answering his math problems. Matthew followed Penelope around as she peered into washrooms and cleaning cupboards giving a full on commentary even when Matthew had walked off. They found a pack of cards and played a ravenous and rapid game of racing demon. Michael gave a look at his watch and called supper time to the other two while Penelope jumped up ready to meet the others. A clattering sound of the 17 other children wafted into their ears and penelope leaped down after them however Matthew was hesitant. Supper was a fun occasion and a friendly boy named Sam came to sit with them. He was a thin, blonde boy with a cloud of freckles upon his nose and they chatted excitedly of all the activities you could do near the village.

They all hurried upstairs after a delicious pudding, a roly poly, and Penelope announced that she'd 'better be off to bed'. Her brothers soon followed suit and before long, Michael was padding into Matthew's room to say good night, something which he had told himself he must do ever since they'd found out the truth about everything.

Upon entering the room, Michael noticed that Matthew was seemingly happier than he was about an hour ago. He assumed Matthew had just thought their circumstances over and realised how lucky they were to actually have a bed right now, but Matthew changed those thoughts by saying,

"I was actually apprehensive, is that the right word Michael?" He looked at his brother for reassurance and Michael nodded his head curtly. "Anyway, I was apprehensive, if you would believe it, but now I know that we will be adopted, quick as a wink—I mean, have you SEEN those other children? Their manners!" He laughed. "I mean with our luck we'll most likely get chosen tomorrow afternoon!" Matthew got into bed happy and hugged his brother. Michael stayed silent. He just didn't have the heart to tell his brother that manners may not be the first thing lonely couples look for and that they might be here a while after all.

13
A New Beginning

DAYS PASSED, AND the Ridgeway children slowly got to grips with their new lifestyle, learning that the other children also liked to watch TV and that the Ridgeway's couldn't always tell them what to do. The children had also had a few meetings with their social worker, Dexter, who was a large, portly man with stubble for a beard which matched his jet black hair. He helped discuss the future and if they would like to be adopted or stay in Cimberly. Without hesitation, they all had chosen to be adopted, so Dexter, had been looking for suitable parents for a day or so now, but with no luck.

Michael normally spent his days shut up in his room, setting himself difficult maths problems, impossible english assignments and even trying to become fluent in Latin. Penelope found this absurd and had given a gigantic yawn on hearing this plan. Because of this penelope and Matthew played cards for many hours, almost becoming as good as a girl named Sophie, whose room was next door to Penelope's. Sophie was so good at cards that other people betted on how fast she would win a match—it was normally around 2 minutes.

Margaret tried her best to make Matthew feel better about the last few weeks, but often had little or no success. She and Matthew would sit for hours in that first room they had all gone to when they arrived at Cimberly, but often couldn't get so much of a sentence out of the youngest Ridgeway. Michael and Penelope were highly worried as well, Matthew had gone off his food and wasn't gloating nearly as much as he used to. They decided that he'd better have extra support meetings with professionals who knew how to deal with his strange behavior.

In the weeks they had been there, very little happened to the Rideways. Others in the orphanage however, having been there for some time, had couples coming in every other day to look at adoption of them. One boy named Jack had already been whirled off by a kind looking lady, however he didn't look too happy. Matthew did not understand this as he would love a new family. He was sitting on his bed having just escaped Penelope's request for a role play with her favourite teddies. Thoughts of breakfast in the manor while Caroline was reading a book or chatting to them entered his mind and his head fell in sadness. He was finding this whole business of a new life extremely difficult and was slightly annoyed at Michael and Penelope who were whirling into the whole process so quickly. He knew he would have to move on some time but felt the only way was to get a new family and Michael didn't seem very optimistic. He stared unfocused at the clean and blue walls before heaving himself up and practising a fake smile for the other two so that they didn't worry. What was he to do today? Maybe he would find a new hobby. Yes that might work. So while Matthew skipped over new activities to participate in over his mind, he padded down those familiar stairs. He planned to sit next to this other girl named Madeline who was in the middle of the process of leaving, she was a pleasant girl and Matthew would be sad to see her go.

When looking back on this period of time, none of the children would remember in the slightest what happened. The days just rolled on, piles of food being packed into their stomachs and yet more card games just filled the hours of empty space. They were happy times. The children became friends with many at the orphanage and they all just became a big united family, laughing and playing throughout the day. Large 2000 piece puzzle filled a very long table on a certain day in july and 9 of the children were huddled round searching for the miniscule pieces. On another day, there was panic in the orphanage when someone fainted after getting a nosebleed. Penelope had squealed so much when she heard that she fell off her chair onto the floor and burst into a chorus of parrot squawks. After this, however she had marvelled in the children's horror and kept calling that an ambulance was on its way or that there was blood all over the evening's meal. And one day, the ridgeways had been introduced to the large grey cat that traipse around staring menacingly at anyone who set eyes on her. She was called tipsy which suited her personality very well as she did seem to be drunk a lot of the time, falling off chairs while her fur stuck up terrorfied.

Penelope and Michael didn't mind the ongoing wait for a family to pick them up as they very much enjoyed life now. It was simple, but ever exciting and new for the children.

Penelope snapped awake with a sharp look round as she recalled the horrible dream of the night before. A few highlighters had begun to walk menacingly towards her before toppling her into an oversized cereal bowl which was full of her beloved teddys covered in milk. She automatically checked the date to see

Tuesday the 14 of August and sprung herself onto a small white desk where she sweeped out her notepad to scribble down the dream she had just remembered. A sharp knock cracked onto her door and by the slow, dull tap she knew it was Michael.

"Come in Michael,"

"How on earth did you know it was me?"

"Well firstly your knock is as dull as poppie's old photo galleries. (poppy being the portly lady to welcome them) and secondly you come in every single morning at precisely 7:47 to say good morning."

"Oh well, I've already had a quick bowl of cereal and sam, that blond boy said this is our village day and that he would take us around."

"Oh lord, shopping, Matthew will enjoy himself." Penelope said in a disgusted voice. She was not a shopper but Matthew rather liked it. Michael was fine with this as that meant matthews christmas present for him was always marvellous.

"Coming down?"

"Yes I suppose I shall, but let me get dressed mind."

"Yes, yes" and with that Michael swung the white washed door shut. Penelope had failed to put her sign up on her door. She was still yet to unpack and her clothes lay splattered around her suitcase much to the disapproval of Michael. Her desk was also messy and you might ask how because Penelope doesn't have much stuff but she always found a way to turn a room into a tip. Penelope stretched a pair of jeans onto her legs and pulled a green sleeved shirt onto her shoulders.

She then wafted through the study and into the cantine, passing Matthew as he went out.

"Matthew, have you heard the plan for today?"

"No, what are we doing?" he said in a slightly depressed voice.

"We're going shopping in town, Sam's taking us so it should be rather enjoyable. I'll just have brecky and then let's go."
"Oh ok, I'll just get my things." Matthew said slightly chirpier.
It was good for Matthew to do something new, it took his mind off things.

Penelope headed towards the cereal table, grabbed a bowl of rice krispies and strolled out to a table with Sophie. She gulped the whole bowl up within two minutes and apologised to Sophie for leaving, before she hurried out. Keeping Michael waiting was not a happy sight.

After 15 minutes, the three Ridgeway's and now Sam, who had come hurtling down thoroughly excited at being the leader of the group, skipped out of the door sending a few reassuring words to Margaret who was slightly worried. This was a feeling that came a lot however because it was like she had a crowd of children under her wing.
Sam strolled in front, taking long and wide steps along the narrow, winding pavement, pointing from side to side talking aloud about the villages nearby.
"Yes, that's where we came from, Tardford, that was where we used to live." Called Penelope and Sam halted not wanting to be insensitive, it had only been a month or so after all. Michael gave a swift glance at Matthew but saw that he was just about OK. The fresh air must have helped, he agreed.

It was a kind looking town. Although it had seemed rather gloomy on the children's arrival; their miserable and nervous glance at the world had probably caused this or maybe just the grey light upon the village on that particular day.

The children had of course quickly passed through this village before the incident, as the three ridgeway children were now calling it, and Penelope told Sam so, clearly unabashed by her own past.

So large and delightful was the village, that the children had a super day ahead of them. Millions of stone tiles created wide paths down towards shops and the supermarket. Sam took them round an odd shop full of large armchairs and huge beds, although Penelope and Matthew marvelled at how soft all the sheets were as they stretched wildly open them while Michael stood, disapproving looks filling his face. Michaels face however changed dramatically into a calm and smug face as the old, wrinkled shop keeper shoved them back onto the busy pavement. Sam, then lead them through a swinging black gate to a bright green park with a pair of swings and a miniature climbing wall. Michael was tempted to have a swing but decided strongly that he was *much* too old for such petty things as playgrounds. Penny once again, completely annihilating all stereotypes, leaped upon the red frame and started to swing back and forth, her legs flailing wildly into the air.

Matthew and Sam clawed onto the climbing wall and Michael gave in, grabbing the cold chain of a swing.

With four flushed faces leaving the park, they hopped into a shop requested by Matthew and all got a small bag of sweets. Michael had been the only sensible one to bring his wallet on leaving Ridgeway manor so reluctantly paid for all, except Sam of course who refused point blank to take money from Michael.

They then shuffled into a game store before Michael hurried into a maths supplies shop waving an arm for the others to join. Penelope, Matthew and Sam didn't stay long and gave the shop one glance before stalking off to leave Michael fixated on a new set of triangular maths equipment.

The day of pure enjoyment ended with an ice cream paid for by Margaret who had hurried out quickly to join them. Matthew walked back to the orphanage a broad grin on his face while he slurped at the chocolate ice cream that started to shine as the sun melted the circular balls of childhood slightly. Penelope nudged Michael and they shared a look of relief while staring at Matthew thoroughly pleased that he was almost back to his original self. Sam was animatedly chatting to Sophie who had joined the group. The strolled through the orphanage door, opened my Margerat and all headed into the study for a board game.

A large supper of shepherds pie followed and all the children slurped down a glass of warm milk before heading off to bed. Penelope as expected threw a bag of things onto her bed and with hardly taking two steps into her room cluttered out and into Michael's room too impatient to warn him with a knock.

"Hellooo, just came in for a chat,"

"I should've guessed," Michael spoke in a bored voice. He left his desk and perched onto his bed almost protecting it from Penelope's messy hands.

"Funny how life has changed so drastically and we are still the same,"

"Yes, I suppose so, I rather like all the change though," pondered Penelope with a nod of the head. They were silent for a second, Michael just staring into space.

"I hope matthews ok, he's been quiet for weeks,"

"Yes, i'm sure he'll come around, the funny thing is i don't remember our parents being very loving," said penelope with a short sniff of amusement

"Yes, one could ask what he is missing,"

"To be fair he's much younger, maybe it's just hard for him to be without parents,"

"Yes, anyway, i might go to sleep, do you mind," said michael

"Oh no, not at all, goodnight," Penelope said without, however, moving in the slightest.

"Um, do you mind going back to your room because i'm going to sleep."

"Oh, you want me to move as well, well alright, Asking quite a lot but ok." said Penelope, confused and slightly annoyed.

"Um goodnight,"

"Yes, night," Penelope called as she took a final spin on michaels chair and waved out grabbing at the handle to shut the door.

14
The Stevens'

ALMOST TWO WHOLE months had passed now, and Michael had a nice little routine setup: wake up, work, breakfast, work, check on siblings, lunch, work, walk and then supper. He was just going up after his breakfast, his usual toast with marmite, to do some work when Margaret stopped him in the corridor.

"Now, Michael?"

"Yes Margaret?"

"Would you mind telling your siblings to come down to the meeting room, Dexter's there, he wants a word."

"Do I come as well?"

"Oh yes dear, hurry along now."

Michael bustled off and into Penelope's room, where she and Matthew were lying on the floor, emerged in yet another game of racing spit, Penelope's favourite. They looked up as he entered.

"Oh hello Michael!" Penelope exclaimed in an oddly happy tone.

"Hello you two. I've just passed Margaret in the corridor and she said to come down to the study as Dexter is there and he wants to have a word"

"Oh alright, come on Matthew" Penelope said in bored tones as she heaved Matthew off the floor by his wrist. She bounded out of the door and Michael could hear her jumping and thumping down the stairs, three at a time! He winced. She could have an accident for all he knew. He swiftly got up, took Matthew's hand and walked out of the room, deliberately stepping carefully down one step at a time as if an invisible judge was there to mark him out of ten.

Penelope was sitting on the familiar squishy red sofa when her brothers arrived. Dexter was on a small footstool and Margaret lingered behind, straightening the cat pictures. Michael smiled weakly at them and steered Matthew towards Dexter.

"Hello boys." Dexter said in his deep, calming voice.

"Good day," said Michael.

"Well, I won't beat about the bush. There is a couple who is interested in taking you on."

There was silence. Matthew clenched his hands into fists; Michael could see that he was trying to contain his excitement.

"What are they like?" Said Michael, breaking the silence as he had so often done back in the cellar.

"Well they are a happily married couple and quite willing to take on a few children!"

"My goodness this *is* good news!"

"When will we meet them?"

"Um tomorrow you'll have a short outing to the park where you will meet them. Margaret will accompany you there of course."

"Great scot, that's in less than 48 hours!" Michael shrieked.

"May we go?" Penelope said, smiling a sort of sickly smile.

Back upstairs, the children chattered nonstop about their future lives. Not even Michael had any depressing thoughts of sadness to contribute about the next day's events.

"I wonder if they'll have a trampoline?!"

"Maybe we'll have a barbecue every Saturday!"

"I hope they have lots of space so I can still do my experiments!"

The rest of the day was a drag. The children had been told not to say anything to the others so that there would be no jealousy. This meant that they had to lie to Sam about their excitement of the coming day, which made Michael feel very uneasy—he didn't like lying. It made him think of his parents.

Finally, it was dinner, and Michael, Penelope and Matthew ate as fast as they could, eager to make tomorrow come sooner. They scurried up to their rooms and flung themselves into bed after saying a hurried goodnight to one another.

The next morning passed in a blur. On the one hand, the children were excited to see the couple, but on the other, what were they going to be like? How would the children make a good impression? Michael was praying to himself that Penelope wouldn't start rambling off about her teddies' wise words of wisdom or about how she liked to squawk like a parrot when feeling happy, and ruin everything!

Margaret hurriedly told them to get their coats on before they left as a light breeze had started to form into a gust and it was quite chilly out. Michael supervised his siblings as they got ready for their new chapter of their life.

As they walked along the pavement, Margaret told them all about the couple, Mr and Mrs Stevens and that they worked in a clothing manufacturer—that was how they had met around 20 years ago. By the time her explanation about them was finished, they were walking into the park. They had only just sat down on a damp park bench when Matthew asked in a husky voice,

"Is that them?"

Two figures were walking towards them, smiles all over their face. Mrs Stevens was a small blonde woman with thin faded eyebrows, a tanned face and bright green eyes. She had a small handbag around her shoulder and was hugging it tightly, clearly excited. She wore long jeans that flowed onto the slightly damp grass and a white shirt that was tucked into her trousers. She stood still, a comforting but scared smile upon her face. They all stood up, Margaret taking Matthew's hand and introduced themselves.

"Hello you three!" Mrs Stevens said excitedly.

"You do look well!"

"Thank you," Matthew replied, clearly taken aback by her warm and friendly tone.

"How are you doing?" Mr Stevens asked.

Mr Stevens, the tall man to have just spoken, was packed into a smart suit, his hair slightly messy and long, running down his neck past his dark brown eyes while smiling at the children. His dark brown skin reflected the sunlight on his hands and his muscular legs led to two large feet bouncing slightly in excitement.

"Fine thanks." Spoke up Michael, in his loud, confident mannar.

Everyone was looking at Penelope, clearly waiting for her to contribute to the conversation.

"It's a nice and blustery day isn't it!" she said, her eyes following a few stray leaves that were whirling around.

Mrs Stevens' smile flickered for a second, but she hitched back on almost immediately and looked at Matthew sympathetically.

"So," Mrs Stevens glanced at Margaret who nodded encouragely. "What do you all enjoy doing?"

"Well, where to start? I enjoy maths problems, english essays, letter writing, and poetry. All quite academical you see *but* that doesn't mean I don't enjoy the occasional game of racing demon."

"How come then you threw a book at my head yesterday when I asked you to join in on a game with me and matthew?!" Shrieked Penelope indignantly.

"Well I was rather busy then Penny—and would you mind using the correct terms by saying 'Matthew and *I*' instead of 'me and Matthew." He smiled smugly.

"Ok, how nice, um how about you, ah, Matthew," spoke Mrs Stevens leaning slightly closer to Matthew.

"Umm, drawing, shopping sometimes, maybe reading?"

"What! I've never seen you draw!" said Penelope. "Wait? Is *that* why you didn't want to play role play with my teddies yesterday?"

"Might have been the reason." Muttered Matthew, scuffing his feet and looking down.

They ended up having lunch with the Stevens'. As they all munched on fish and chips, the couple told the children all about their holidays abroad in Africa and America. They also told them about their holiday home in Cornwall where they often made homemade ice cream. This made Penelope very excited. She liked the idea of a homemade ice cream on her holidays.

Hours passed and the children continued getting to know the Stevens' and vice versa. They were all having a lovely time when Margaret checked her watch. Her eyes widened slightly and she said "Oh goodness! We've completely run out of time! Could you send an email to Dexter saying your thoughts—I've got to get these three back for supper by 6 and I need to pop to the shops before that, sorry children you will have to come."

"Ah, well, see you children!"

Mr Stevens ruffled Matthew's hair and with a haughty nod, Mrs Stevens smoothed her blouse down and walked off, taking her husband's arm.

As the two shadows strolled away, deep in conversation, the three children turned round and began to follow Margaret towards a large supermarket.

"I think that went well, we shall see how they feel in a few days." spoke up Margaret keen to keep the children excited.

"Yes I suppose so, I don't think I made a very good impression, maybe I should have mentioned learning Latin."

"Oh I don't think so, let's just keep our fingers crossed." Margaret said while grabbing Matthew's hand in a motherly fashion.

"I hope they do become our parents, they seemed very nice." said Matthew very joyfully. Penelope however rolled her eyes and thought privately that they could have done a lot better.

Margaret led them into a shop while pleading words of comfort that they would only be twenty minutes. Penelope, Michael and Matthew followed obediently and grabbed a few ingredients commanded by Margaret. They raced around the large hall, down the isles and up towards the counter. Matthew, while squinting wildly for the pasta, turned his head quickly as he spied out of the corner of his eye, the Stevens picking out some sausages. They looked towards him and gave a quick smile and a wave, before hurriedly strolling off. He smiled back, his tummy glowing in joy. Would they actually be his parents. He hoped so, very much.

The rest of the group had been oblivious to the second appearance of the Stevens and Matthew didn't tell them. He wanted to keep this meeting as his own. They huddled at the counter, Margerat in front, deep in her purse. The money was exchanged, and with a short 'thank you' to the kind shopkeeper, The group of four clattered out of the large shop, and back onto the street.

The light around them started to fade and billowing clouds formed above their heads, spitting rain dropping gently onto their hair. A car's lights blinded the four figures momentarily and sped past. Matthew was swinging onto the hand of Margaret's while jumping high into the small puddles formed in the dents of the tarmac. They headed up a few stairs and finally arrived in the warm corridor, the children ruffling their heads dry.

Margaret shared a kind word to the three and walked swiftly towards her office, saying hello to a small boy who was running past. Matthew clopped upstairs and onto his bed with a positive mindset,

"How could they not want us?" he thought and with that he seized his drawing pad and started on a new drawing of a large and cosy house now with two people standing outside. A blonde, short lady and a tall, long haired man. He was sure the Stevens would be his new parents. Was sure he would have a new and perfect life by next week.

*   *   *

A few days followed, anticipation sketched upon the children's faces. A message from Dexter had still not arrived and the children, Matthew especially, were becoming slightly worried. This excitement and distress however, caused three days of almost no activity. The children just sat in the study, cards in front of them, a game in process, yet not being played. Matthew was bent over his drawing pad while Penelope just mouthed different words towards her pink teddy that was gripped in front of her nose. By this time, any children that were momentarily keen to play with them, had left in a huff, bored by all the silence. Only Sam stayed, staring blankly out of the window unable to think of anything better to do.

A call for supper echoed around the room on the third day of this slump and the children leapt at something to do and strolled through the narrow corridor, past the crowd of cat pictures and into the canteen to find their supper laid out on the table.

It was tomato soup and Penelope's face showed pure hatred for the food and a look that described the feeling that she would have much rather sit in the study with her teddy. The rest of the children were red in the face with muddy knees from playing football in the back garden and were ripping at the large slices of bread set aside their bowls.

The garden was a pleasant space with two goals either end of a small area of grass and a selection of wheels and tubes of wood, designed as an obstacle course for the children. It had spindly wooden fences all around and a little gate that was firmly locked at all times although the children highly doubted anyone would want to escape.

The ridgeway children were not a sporty type so did not venture into the garden often, however Matthew was to be found there on a rare chance, maybe drawing a tree or a bunch of flowers. Michael however stayed away from the whole area, the idea of muddy knees just making him sqirm. Chess was the sport for him.

15

A Chance for Matthew

MATTHEW AWOKE, THE time being about 8 o'clock on a Saturday morning halfway through August, the same feeling of butterflies in his stomach. As he sat on his bed, shoving a pair of socks onto his feet a knock on the door came. Matthew, expecting it to be Michael or Penelope yelled 'come in' and was surprised to find Margaret bobbing her head between the door.

"Do you mind coming down to the study, Dexter has come to see you,"

"Are Penelope and Michael there?"

"Um, no, he's asked for just you." said Margaret sensitively. Matthew's face fell into a bemused expression and muttered something about being there in 5 minutes.

Matthew sat in front of Dexter, not really listening to what he was saying. He knew why he was here—these dull happy learning classes. He nodded in all the right moments and started wondering about the ice cream he would pile into his stomach tonight—it was Sunday evening and everyone had ice cream at supper then.

"So would you be okay with that Matthew?" asked Dexter. Matthew suddenly snapped into focus. He was sure to be in trouble if he said he hadn't been listening.

"Oh yes!" he said enthusiastically. He didn't really care what happened as long as he got out of this boring meeting quickl, as he thought he was about to drop off!

"But are you sure Michael and Penelope would be okay with it as well?" Asked Dexter, looking at Matthew in concern.

"Yes, yes they'll be fine with it—I'm sure!" Said Matthew dismissively. 'They'll be fine with anything if you just hurry up' he thought.

"Ok then Matthew. See you tomorrow with the Stevens' then!"

Matthew left in a hurry, eager to get back to his drawing, the last few words spoken by Dexter not drifting directly to matthews ears. He had gotten into this whole drawing hobby thoroughly since he'd first met the Stevens' and was keen to carry on.

Next day, Matthew walked glumly into the meeting, ready for another hour bored out of his wits. He was most surprised to see Mr and Mrs Stevens there, waiting for him expectantly.

"Err, hello?" Matthew said hesitantly.

"Hello dear Matthew!" Mrs Stevens said in a rich, warm voice.

"Ready to leave then dear?"

"What!, what do you mean, what about penelope and matthew?" yelled Matthew in distress, his hands reaching for the back of the chair just to have something so grab onto.

"Mr and Mrs Stevens just want to take you out for a couple of hours to the park or a few shops." said dexter in a calm, reassuring voice. Mr and Mrs Stevens looked confused and very worried.

"Don't you remember me telling you all this yesterday?" carried on Dexter.

"Umm, it wasn't really listening, sorry, what did you say, what's happening?"

"Oh well it's pretty important, you see Mr and Mrs Stevens felt they would like younger children so chose you to adopt and come home with them but not Penelope and Michael."

"What!" said Matthew in a shaky voice, "I have to leave them?"

"You don't have to do anything, it's up to you." piped up Mr Stevens in a soothing voice.

"Yes, why don't you go with them today and then we can talk about it more when you come back." spoke Dexter.

"Um, ok"

"You don't have to come now, don't worry." whispered Mrs Stevens in worry

"No, I'll come, I'd like to."

"Well that's settled, I'll see you at around two back here." Dexter finalised leading the three out.

"Have fun Matthew," he called as they left and Matthew gave him a quick but faltery smile.

Once Matthew was out and about, he was beginning to rather enjoy himself. For once he was the centre of attention to Mr and Mrs Stevens and it felt lovely having two people that cared for him so much. They swung for about 20 minutes straight on the swings before going to a sweet stall, toy shop and a small walk down by a river. Matthew strolled along side the two grownups talking for ages about how he came to be at the orphanage whilst staring around at the rippling, whirling water that bubbled down the sloppy muddy river bed and the large overhanging, elegant trees that swung over his head, waving in the soft breeze while knocking of the odd leaf or drop of rain onto his head.

They all crept over a bridge to play poo sticks and Matthew roared with laughter as the two grownups sticks got stuck in the green weeds. They strolled all the way back to a little sandwich van seeing a herd of ducks waddling across the path and grabbed a few sandwiches.

By ten to two matthew had forgotten all about the awkwardness between him and his two siblings and was ready to run off with the couple, however, as he strolled through the orphanage door, saying goodbye to mr and mrs stevens, the guilt and sadness at the prospect of leaving Penelope and Michael flooded back hard and his mind returned to the truth and undeniable sadness of the present.

He got into the warm hall, hanging up his coat on a peg and scurried upstairs, eager for his sketch pad—it was the only thing that would empty his mind after his full morning.

He had settled himself on his bed, colouring pencils askew and was getting into sketching a cherry blossom tree when his bedroom door flew open with a crash.

"Hey Penelope." He said, without looking up. No one in their right mind would open a door like that!

"Hi Matthew!" Came her reply.

"I was just wondering where you were earlier."

Matthew looked up. Michael was hovering behind Penelope as well. He gulped.

"I was out." he said simply.

"With whom may i ask?" Questioned Michael, looking as though he would ask even without permission.

"The S—Stevens'" muttered Matthew.

"WHAT!" Screamed his siblings.

"Why weren't we invited?" inquired Penelope.

"Well, I was sort of not listening in my meeting with Dexter yesterday and it turned out I had agreed to come with them today." Matthew whimpered, his voice drowning through the now thick and compressed air that surrounded the small room.

"I CAN'T BELIEVE THIS!" Screamed Penelope but Michael shushed her.

"Did you enjoy yourself Matthew?" He asked, his quiet voice contrasting with Penelope's yell.

"Err I actually did thanks Michael." He glanced at Penelope,

"but i would have had more fun if you two had been with me" He said quickly.

"I can't believe this." Penelope said again in a shaking voice. She turned and walked out. They heard her slamming her bedroom door shut.

"Don't worry about her." Michael said reassuringly.

"Now, you said you had a good time right?" Matthew nodded.

"Well then, the Stevens' don't want me and Penelope." Matthew opened his mouth in protest but Michael interrupted him with

"I KNOW they don't Matthew. So, you like them. Go with them. Start a new life."

"I don't want to leave you Michael!"

"Penelope and I are holding you back, no one wants two nearly teenage twins nowadays. But people want you. You are a sweet and innocent 8 year old."

"I won't leave you two!"

"You've got to." Said Michael, suddenly stern.

"You wont get out of here if you don't start taking these chances. There might not be another one Matthew."

He gave his brother a quick hug and left the room, so that Matthew wouldn't have to see the tears forming in Michael's eyes.

Matthew was left in deep thought, he had always shown such admiration and respect for michael that he was convinced that michael must be right. He did love the Stevens and would much rather have a new life than the orphanage but then again what about Penelope's reaction?

Matthew stayed in his room for the rest of the afternoon, thoughts rushing and whirling in his head like a million screams even though the room was full of pure silence. He just didn't know what to do. He now had a headache and returned absentmindedly back to his drawing. He knew he must say yes, it was too big an opportunity and Michael had said he should.

6 oclock came and he hovered down stairs, his head full yet empty. The long, messy hair of penelope waved around the door to the cantine just as he turned off the stairs, he knew she was ignoring him.

Supper was a silent affair, the children either deep in thought or determined not to talk. The pesto pasta was slowly engulfed and he ate up a small apple before being called by Margaret to come.

Matthew walked beside her, his eyes unfocused and tired. Dexter welcomed him with a shake of the arm. He sat once again opposite Matthew and went on about this big opportunity and why it was the right thing to do. Then, 20 long minutes having gone, the question that Matthew had been waiting for arrived.

"So, how about it, do you want to go with Mr and Mrs Stevens?."

There was a silence, soft chirps of chatter from supper ringing faintly in the background. Matthew's face was pale and blank.

With one short open of the mouth matthew said
"Yes."

The decision was made and Dexter made a final word about all the paperwork and that he was to leave on the morning of the 19th. two days time. Dexter led Matthew out and he headed quickly up to his room not wanting to make eye contact with anyone or anything.

They all slept badly that night, Penelope and Michael not knowing whether Matthew was going or not, and what they were ever to do without him. When morning came the awkward conversation as expected commenced. It was short but emotional. Few words were said and Penelope left quite soon after the start. Michael was kind and comforting but timid and mostly silent. He muttered something of heading down for lunch and left Matthew alone to ponder his thoughts.

The following day acted as pretty much the same. Hardly any talk. Hardly any contact. Matthew slowly and hesitantly packed up his few possessions and after another meeting with Dexter was feeling ready to crouch into his own shell not wanting to carry on.

Supper was 15 minutes away and Penelope was crashing around in her room, trying not to think about the coming events. She didn't want to go on without her younger brother but also didn't want to restrict his future by being selfish. She slumped down, deeply sad not knowing what would happen and fearing the next day. How would she cope?

Another awkward dinner followed and another broken up sleep commenced. But finally the facts had definitely sunk into all three of them. Matthew was leaving, he was starting a new life. Three would become two.

*   *   *

Matthew awoke. It took him a few seconds to realise why he felt so uneasy. He stared wildly around and caught sight of his bags, all packed and ready for his departure later that morning. He gulped hard and swung his legs out of bed, they were steel, unable to bend.

After hurriedly pulling on his clothes, he pattered downstairs for a breakfast of weetabix and cold milk. He tried not to think about Penelope's refusal to talk to him ever since he had come back after that glorious morning with the Stevens'.

After breakfast, he rushed upstairs, wanting to be ready when his new family would arrive. He placed his sketch pad carefully into his train patterned suitcase and zipped it shut, sighing.

A knock on the door interrupted his thoughts on his new home. It was Penelope. Her eyes were red and her hair was in it's usual birdsnest.

"I just came to say," she began, but then raced forwards and pulled Matthew into a warm embrace.

"Good luck." she whispered into his hair.

"You'll have an amazing time." and she slipped a note into his jean pocket.

"Thanks," Matthew replied. Looking up for a second into her eyes.

When they broke apart Penelope's jumper was rather wet where Matthew's face had been. He turned away, embarrassed.

"Goodbye," Penelope said and she slowly, shakily stepped out of his room pressing his door reluctantly shut.

12:00 o'clock came and Matthew was gripping his suitcase. His hand was slippery with sweat so he wiped it on his new jeans that Michael had recently bought him as a surprise. He looked down at his muddy trainers and shuddered. He slid downstairs while saying a few words of farewell and thanks to Margaret. His voice seemed to have stopped working. The sound ebbing away from his mouth in a quiet and Insinsear voice. But Margerat knew how grateful he was. She gave him a quick hug and a weak smile before moving into stillness, her whole body fading into the white wall.

Michael and Penelope were atop the stairs looking down on the scene. Their tears had stopped now. They were frozen in a hug, so empty with feeling.

A knock came. The Stevens pulled open the door and Matthew's eyes set onto the kind couple. They beckoned him forward and he stepped out the door, giving a sweeping look behind him at the other two.

"Are you ready to go?"

"Yes,"

The group of three walked out. The door shut. There was silence.

16
A Day at School

THE SCENE FROZE like a pause button had just been pressed. Particles of air stopped, breathing faltered. The ringing echo of the shutting door was loud in Penelope and Michael's ears. Margaret was still, quiet.

And then it happened. A loud, banging crash came and a flash of movement flew across the floor. Shrieks erupted from Margaret as the door repeatedly banged against white wall. Matthew had exploded through the door running at his brother and sister and they had welcomed him into a large, warm hug. The three heads curled together, tears burst from the Ridgeway's eyes and Matthew gave a muffled cry into Penelope shoulder

"I'm never leaving, we either all go or none of us."

"Oh Matthew."

The few words had said all that needed to be said and all three, now grinning madly clattered up the stairs.

"How about a game of racing demons?"

"Yes but we are playing by my rules? That means the teddies play." Called Penelope, her original character filling her bones in a flash. Penelope, Michael and Matthew had gone without one look back to leave Margerat in a frozen laugh, Dexter slightly uncomfortable and Mr and Mrs Stevens shocked out of their wits a few metres outside the door.

"I'm so sorry Mr and Mrs Stevens, I don't know what to say. Chattered Dexter, nervous and slightly guilty.

"No no, you can't just split a family."

"Thank you for all your time."

And with that Mr and Mrs Stevens slightly shakily but proud of their decision left down the stairs, the clip of their shoes fading into the background.

"Well, what a few hours!" Margaret said, breaking the soft silence and giving an all knowing look towards dexter.

"Right, come into my office, we have some things to discuss."

"Yes, my job is certainly not done with these children." And with a weak smile towards Dexter she swiftly walked towards a white washed door into a dark blue and silver office, Dexter following business like after her.

A babbling, bubbling, bouncing chatter jumped wildly from the children's mouth as they flicked and flapped cards onto the small tilting wooden table. Their knees were pressing hard into the rough, creme carpet while Penelope shrieked phrases like 'well quite' and 'oh darn, oh darn, oh darn'. The two boys were bent low focused, muttering numbers and suits beneath their noses. Michaels eyes were flashing around the table as Matthew's hands paced round picking up and putting down cards. Penelope's teddies, who sat side by side at the other end of the table, cards laid out in front of their noses, with their stuffed necks folding under the weight of their foam filled heads, had not gained a point. Penelope, however, was still hopeful for her rainbow coloured friends and collapsed onto her back clearly tired of the game while feeling her beloved teddies would win without a doubt.

"Yes, king."

"Out."

And the game was over, Michael and Matthew heaving a sigh of Relief before slumping down. Michael had a smug look around at the other two while Matthew looked slightly glum but still happy. Penelope snapped up and with a call said

"Oh Michael, well done,"

"But Matthew got a king, so it might be close."

Penelope and Michael huffed into a conversation of what they were going to do this week. Matthew was once again hunched.

"Right. Here are the scores:

In third Penelope with minus 15

In second well me with 86

And in third, yes yes alright, Matthew with 113."

Michael gave a cheer and they all leapt up slowly wandering down the stairs, a wafting smell of sausages waving up their nostrils.

The shining sun had long gone when all three bumped and swung upstairs talking nonstop. Their bellies were wedged with food from the supper before and there faces were slightly red with sweat from the rollercoaster of emotions. It had been a pleasant time with happy words from all the other children of the joy that

Matthew would still be with them at the orphanage. Matthew was very glad he was staying. He did love it here and he was with his sibling, that was what mattered. Many yawns followed as the three children all walked into Matthew's room ready to help unpack his many belongings.

"I'm so glad you're back Matthew." Said Michael, smoothing out his brother's sketchbook—it had become crumpled in Matthews haste to get back inside.

"So am I." Matthew, smiled weakly. It had been a tiring couple of hours.

"I don't know if Margaret told you Matthew," began Michael,

"But term starts on Monday ."

"Oh goody, I've been missing Mr Harris." Said Matthew, moving forwards to straighten his pencils that Penelope had laid out on his desk.

"Err, no Matthew, we're going to a public primary school."

"What?!"

"It's true Matthew," Penelope said, "look at our uniform—it's so exciting!" She held out green jumpers which each had a circular logo saying, 'Cimberly Primary School' sewed in navy thread.

"But I don't know how to go to a proper school! I don't know how to make friends!"

"Look it will be fine, we will face it on Monday, let's not think about it now,"

"Yes, you up for some cheat?" said Penelope with a raise of the eye brows. Matthew gave a small laugh as Penelope now looked like a slightly plastic cartoon. They settled down onto the floor and Michael pulled out a messy pile of cards and put them on the floor. Penelope had been the one to clear them away last time.

9 o'clock came, and the children were back in their rooms, chatting a quick goodnight. Matthew collapsed in his bed looking straight up at the blank ceiling, his brain working madly. School? After all that had just happened?

The morning of Monday came and Penelope, Michael and Matthew were whipping hurriedly school uniforms onto their bodies while toothbrushes were gripped in their mouths.

The day before had been a mediocre one, the children had done very little except stressfully get all their things ready for the next day. By night time, Michael of course had a small pile of his folded uniform beside his bed and a small bag with pencil case as well.

This morning however, Michael was stressed, his hair on end, eyes bulging. They all gulped up a bowl of cereal and Margaret led them softly towards the door, a few other children yapping behind them.

The school was a grey one with a concrete playground and tiled stairs that led to a depressing white door. The windows were smudged and dirty looking like they had not been cleaned for several months. Michael, Penelope and Matthew followed the headmistress as she led them in. The head of Cimberley Primary School was a rounded, well blossomed woman who had most experience from new children as they had all come and gone from the orphanage. Her name was Mrs Burch. Margaret had left them swiftly at the gate. They stared around looking at everything from the pitiful library to the climbing frame seated in the school field.

Michael was very dissatisfied with the library, as it had books he'd read and finished when he was Matthew's age but none he was reading now, like 'War and Peace'. Penelope was very interested in the climbing frame but nothing much else. Matthew, who had been so excited about the art rooms (he'd read many books about schools) was most displeased that there was none.

"Oh no dear, we do our art work in the same classrooms where we do everything else." Was the reply when Matthew had timidly asked. The classrooms all looked exactly the same. Red metal tables, creme, slightly speckled walls and small square seating area with large blue boxes hidden underneath.

Matthew was dropped off in a classroom called 'Kingfishers' whilst Penelope and Michael were placed in a classroom called 'Owls' (the twins were at the top of the school which made them feel very superior). Penelope and Michael strolled towards the door confidently but when entering Michael froze like in slow motion and his head tilted downwards, embarrassed. Penelope however bounded in and walked over to a twin table. Michael slowly followed flashing quick glances at all the children gabbling to each other.

As he just began to tilt into the spindle chair, a tall, long legged lady stalked into the room, a smart knee length skirt around her waist.

"Right, morning everyone, I am Miss Points" she said in a strong voice signalling a deathly silence in the classroom.

"She doesn't seem too happy," Michael muttered

"Yes, she could do with a fun teddy on her desk, it would brighten up the whole classroom," Penelope whispered quickly.

"Mathematics," she said syllable by syllable, crashing a large pile of textbooks onto the table. After this, she whipped around the classroom like a small giraffe doing ballet, or at least that's what Penelope thought, slipping sheets of paper onto the children's desks.

"Right, we are doing a test,"

These words were answered with a chorus of mumbling and deep sighing. This was obviously done often, as the children started automatically grabbing a pen, pencil and rubber.

Penelope stared at the 1st question which was, 'Number 1, calculate the value of X when Z=12 and N=10'. She buried her face in her hands, sighing deeply and crashed her pen onto the table in boredom.

"Right shh now, and get on, you have 35 minutes," she said.

Penelope, with a drooling face of displeasure, joined in with the others, picking up the pen, while Michael snatched at the paper, extremely focused and hunched over to start scribbling down his answers.

34 minutes later found a shriek from the teacher that the test was over and she scurried over to pick up all of the sheets. The children sat silent, ready for whatever might come next. The teacher's eyes flashed down the pages, her hands flicking through.

"Now now, who is this Michael Ridgeway?" she said haltingly on a page. Michael hand shakily raised into the air.

"Very good, very good, yes full marks. Well done." Michaels cheeks flushed with a slightly proud look and he worked hard to not look smug.

The day slowly passed, French, History and PE dragging on, Penelope's eyes sunken and deeply bored. They caught up with Matthew on the concrete playground for break. They didn't talk much, but Matthew seemed to be struggling through the day, not too miserable. Penelope jumped a hopscotch as Michael stood awkwardly, arms crossed looking around and the crowds of children.

At lunch time, Penelope ran into the hall to grab three seats next to each other whilst Michael hurried off to fetch Matthew from his class. When everyone had snatched a tray from the mounting pile before the array of greasy food, Michael piled food onto Matthew and Penelope's plates and told their disgusted faces that they needed to have strength before their next lesson, he then led the way back to their seats.

They were all settled down and about to dig into their food (if you would call it edible), when two teachers clapped their hands together for attention, standing up at the same time. One of the teachers was Mrs Burch, easily recognizable with a fruity orange scarf wrapped around her, but the other one no one recognized. A stern looking man with a wrinkled forehead and a shiny suit, he looked at the children as if they were all vermin.

"It has come to my attention," said Mrs Burch, as the dining hall became silent.

"And mine!" The man butted in.

"Oh yes, and Mr Downs'." She smiled, the falseness not being seen by his long, dissatisfied face.

"That there was lots of running and pushing on the way to Lunch Hall. Now, you all know that this is STRICTLY FORBIDDEN as this school simply can't afford to have any more court cases put against them for injuries. So please." She stared hard at Penelope who was now fishing through her pasta with her fingers,

"don't do it again." The teachers both sat down at their table and the general noise of chatter restarted. Penelope continued to search her pasta until she found a ghastly grey hair concealed in one of the pieces, this resulting in an early finish of lunch for the children.

English came next and Penelope's chin almost slapped onto the table in annoyance as Mrs Points pointed towards the board at a 36 slide power point of Macbeth. Titled, Soliloquies.

After a dull and boring lesson where Miss Points found it necessary to pick on everyone in the class for the answers, apart from Michael, the clock in the corner showed that it was five minutes to the end of the day. Michael and Penelope joined the rest of the class in hurriedly stuffing all their belongings into their bags while Miss Points screamed at the top of her lungs "Have I asked you to pack up?" and

"it doesn't need discussion!"

The school bell rang and the children ran towards the gate and flung themselves towards Margaret, who was waiting expectantly, talking to another Mother.

"Hello you three! Tell me all about your day when we get back." she said, ruffling Matthews hair and taking his hand.

They all waited a few more minutes for the other children to arrive, as Michael, Penelope and Matthew were not the only ones who attended the Primary School from the orphanage. Sam, Sophie and another girl named Gwen who had arrived at the orphanage a few days before, were all there.

The days of school slowly drifted by and Matthew and Penelope arrived back each day more tired and bored than before. One day, on arriving back at the orphanage, Penelope simply face planted, her hair rippling behind her onto the bed where she lay for the next hour. The day before, Penelope's neck had swung back, her mouth open wide and a slow rumbling breath had started to drag out of her before Michael gave her a sharp nudge which brought her back to earth. Michael in contrast to this, came home each day quoting little parts of random scottish plays or spending the whole of supper speaking French. Matthew and Penelope having realised this, cleverly just didn't speak to Michael enabling him to answer in what Penelope called jiberish. He also had a habit of quizzing Penelope on the day's work which infuriated her so much that she locked her bedroom door. Matthew was quiet about school but did mention to Margaret about the friends he had made. It sounded like quite a few in the first three days which Michael found very annoying as the only people he could call friends were penelope and most of the teachers. Penelope was surprised he didn't hop into the staff room at break.

Friday finally came and Matthew was thrilled at the news that his class had received an extended break. He, with 20 other classmates, sprinted round playing stuck in the mud. Penelope, having seen this, sighed deeply, her fist on her cheek staring down at the history work about Henry VIII's wifes. She had always thought there were 5 but apparently was wrong. Drama was after break. This was one subject that Michael did not immediately excel in. Penelope wasn't much good either as she believed she was too high in acting to study lines so when they had to perform a short play changed the whole story line. This moment didn't do wonders for her amount of friends, Michael even ignoring her for several minutes. Lunch came at half past twelve and Penelope and Michael strolled into the white washed dining hall to find Matthew seated at a full table.

"well it seems he has other people to sit with now." said Michael, a tad jealous.

"Oh no, I'm sure there's a little room, let's just squeeze in."

She started to walk over but Michael grabbed her and with a short 'no', led her the other direction towards another table. They gobbled up their beans on toast.

After lunch, Matthew trouped back to his class with his gaggle of friends, ready to enjoy some relaxing storytime read by his kind teacher, Mr Fletcher. Penelope and Michael walked back to Owls class, ready to endure a lesson on Science, which was taught by Miss Points and consisted of not doing experiments, but writing essays on the history of the atom!

Their day finally ended and with the prospect of the weekend, Penelope skipped off to the gate, oblivious to the stares around her. They chattered on the way home about the day as they automatically strolled the dark grey pavements and the slightly muddy paths. The door to the orphanage arrived into focus and they barged through it after Margaret had grabbed at her bag, pulled out the key and opened the door.

A couple of hours after they'd arrived home, their game of Racing Demon was interrupted by a sharp bang of the front door. Dexter had arrived. He called the three children into the office, placing a hand on Matthew's shoulder as they all trouped in.

"Sit down." he smiled at them all and sat himself on a footstool as they all scrambled onto the sofas.

"Now, I don't want you all to get too excited, but," he looked at the children who stared back.

"There's a couple who's interested to meet you."

17

A New Couple

A BUSTLING, BUSY woman with bright hazel eyes, a thin but kind smile and shoulder length, dark brown hair, stood at a large wooden island with oversized metal hinges and a large black hob. She wore a long patterned apron and two light grey slippers on her feet. After flashing back from a fazed day dream, she hurried towards a large fridge and pulled it open to grab some mustard. In an automatic little spin, she grabbed a spoon and gouged a spoonful into the large metal pan, creating a faint sizzle.

Her phone lay just beside a large bottle of olive oil with loud words of 'The Archers' ringing out. It was a large pleasant room with little, old wooden tables and two comfy armchairs. On one of these, lay a small, golden dog curved in a relaxed position, her eyes shut, a gentle breath blowing from her wet, black nose. Drops of rain started to creep onto the vintage window frames and with one glance outdoors from the woman, she shrieked and rushed out, slipping into some wellies before running out into the large, slightly overgrown garden muttering about the washing. As the door lay open, cold air waving through it, another door at the other end of the room, just beside the lazy dog flew open and a lumbering man walked in, phone in his hand, talking rapidly.

With a few words of formal goodbye he put his phone onto a round table. The dog bounded down to greet him and he bent low to stroke the small, loving creature. Silence was broken with a loud bang as the door shut and Suzy Taylor, the lady who had five minutes ago been quietly listening to The Archer's heaved into the door, flushed with a huge mound of clothes in her hands.

"oh well done, i was just about to go out myself."

"Oh no dont worry, right shall we go in fifteen. How was work?"

"Oh yes fine. Let me just go to the loo,"

"Alright, oh, i'm a bit nervous. I'll just get my bag. Shall we go in the mini."

"Yep." said brad taylor, the loving husband of suzy had he strolled quickly up the stairs. Suzy pulled her apron off and gave her hair a quick brush. She had never been more nervous but with a pause of 'the archers' and a last gulp of coffee she grabbed the car key and headed out.

*　　　*　　　*

Back in cimberly, there was shocked silence. No one had been expecting this, not even Michael!

"How do we know it won't turn out like the last one?" asked Matthew timidly, giving a little shiver. He still suffered from nightmares about being taken away from his siblings.

"Now, Matthew I'm going to tell you the truth." Dexter said kneeling down in front of Matthew and looking into his face.

"We don't know, we don't know if they are going to turn out like the Stevens' but we can only hope."

"I don't want to do it." Matthew said defiantly.

"Not if i'm going to get split up from you two again."

"We don't know that Matthew!" Michael put in, his arm around his brother, hugging him close,

"but you don't want to stay here forever, honestly?"

"I'd rather stay here than be split up Michael." said Matthew.

"Well, I'll give you all a chance to talk it over with yourselves," said Dexter kindly,

"See you in the meeting to discuss your decision tomorrow morning." he shooed the children out of the room, saying he needed to get down to do some work.

Back upstairs, the children talked over the pros and cons of seeing the couple. Michael made a list, eager to be organised.

"So, pros: we get a new family, we get out of this place, we get more presents at Christmas and Birthdays, we get to move schools or get another Tutor, we get to prove to our parents that we don't need them or their money! This pro side could go on for a while Matthew!" said Michael. Matthew rolled his eyes.

"Let's go onto the cons then Michael."

"Ok, cons: we might get our hopes and dreams bashed, they might be horrible, they might leave us, we might stay in this place longer, well, that's about it isnt it Matthew?"

"I suppose."

"And Matthew", butted in Penelope,

"who knows if they'll want you? They might want me for all we know. I mean to say, it's a bit full of yourself to automatically think they'll only want you."

"Oh Penny."

The children sat having talked themselves into silence, Matthew was still apprehensive but Penelope and Michael were slightly excited.

Saturday arrived and the clocks hit 9 to find Penelope and Matthew still fast asleep. Michael however, having been excited about the prospect of meeting their future parents, once they had said yes this morning, was awake by 7:13 exactly and had been planning and concentrating on how to impress the parents on whatever day they would finally meet. Matthew awoke, butterflies bursting out of his tummy, his eyes snappy and nervous for the day ahead. penelope, the time reaching 9:30 jerked awake before prancing down to the other two at breakfast.

They grouped into the office, and having told Dexter that they would like to meet the couple, sat down, ready to listen to whatever Dexter told them.

"So, they are called Susie and Brad Taylor and they have been married for 15 years but are unable to have children despite their efforts to start a family." began Dexter, looking at the children's eager faces.

"What are their personalities like?" Asked Michael, taking notes with his fountain pen.

"Well I know Susie isn't very sporty, but she's very organised and she loves cooking- so you are all sure to get some good suppers."

"Jolly good!"

"And Brad?"

"Well Brad is the oldest of 6, a family man and an undercover policeman." Dexter said, checking his notes,

"yes, he's a policeman, so mind your P's and Q's when you're around him!" He grinned.

10 minutes later the three children skipped out of the office, feeling fairly excited. They started to babble enthusiastically and Matthew's view on the subject had thoroughly changed. The rest of the day rippled past with Sam and Sophie taking them out to town, where they all dipped their feet into the small stream while playing a game of poo sticks taught by Matthew. To Margaret, giving into their pleas for her to play racing demon with them. Sophie obviously won again.

A special treat was held for the children of the orphanage that night in the shape of a bonfire in the back garden. The Ridgeways had never really seen one before and Matthew gazed, transfixed at the roaring, waving flames that licked slowly at the blackened bark.

Matthew's eyes were large and glassy with the bursts of orange, red and yellow highlighted softly in his iris. Specks of red leapt out of the huge, burning mass and all the children gave a crackling roar of excitement as Margaret threw on a log. Marshmallows came round next and Penelope frantically raced round trying to find the perfect stick. It took her two whole minutes of picking up sticks, measuring them, testing their strength and then putting them down before she found the right one. In fact, she had never looked more like Michael as she did this. The children munched and chewed at the stringy marshmallows filling their mouths and slowly drifted into a daze. They heaved their heavy bones gradually and heavily up the stairs and fell asleep in the few seconds after falling into bed.

*   *   *

The next morning dawned a bright one. Dew settled on the grass, creating a glassy effect on all the spider webs that circled the front door. Michael and Matthew sat on the sofa, dressed in their best clothes, a dark blue tie and blazer for Michael and a smart polo neck for Matthew.

They yelled up the stairs for Penelope to hurry up and finally she emerged, ripping a brush down her thick blonde hair while wearing a grin which paired nicely with her smartest dungarees, which were patched and faded. The morning passed in a blur, the three children sitting smartly by the window that looked out over the street, their hearts pumping faster every time a car slowed down, thinking it would be the Taylor's. It never was.

"They're not going to be early," Michael reassured his siblings for what felt like the tenth time.

"I mean to say, they are due at 11 and it's only half past ten!"

"I suppose." muttered Matthew, twiddling his thumbs.

"I propose that we all play a game of cards!" Penelope said suddenly.

"That's one of your best ideas yet Penny! It'll show the Taylor's that we're well rounded children who have lovely hobbies and aren't obsessed with screens!" called Michael

"Well we aren't, i mean i may like the odd documentary but who doesn't." said Matthew.

"Well, Michael, I wasn't thinking like that!" Said Penelope.

"I was just bored of sitting in silence and looking at cars! I mean, is that what you call fun?"

As Michael dealt cards, he raised a finger in surprise.

"Right, we have now reached 160 rounds of racing demon since we came to the orphanage."

"What, you have been counting?"

"Why, yes"

The doorbell finally rang, interrupting their future argument. An irritating melody rang through the house which annoyed everyone apart from Penelope, who had a little dance she always did when it sounded. She did it now, grinning wildly. Michael pulled her down quickly. He didn't want Penelope to ruin things and couldn't help but quickly place the cards in a smart pile.

A woman swiftly walked in, leading a man in by his arm. She glanced around at the children and gave a swift smile before she carried on walking towards the office, knocking first and then entering. The door slammed behind them, blocking any conversation that would have leaked out.

Ten minutes later, the children having sat silent and excited for the past few moments, Dexter opened the door, his dark brown eyes and freckled face heading towards the children.

"Come you three, they want to meet you."

The three children gripped each other's arms, took a large gulp and sprang up, creeping towards the door. The office that the children had so often fallen into deep boredom looked slightly different. Three circular blue chairs sat in front of them with three others on the opposite side of a small, low wooden table, two of them filled by a kind faced woman with dark brown hair and a tall, smiling man. Dexter sat down and welcomed the children onto the seats. They settled down stiffly and looked up, staring into the two pairs of hazelnut eyes.

"So this is Penelope, Michael and Matthew. And children, this is Suzy and Brad Taylor"

"Hello, how are you, how's school, have you just started?" Said Suzy, starting the conversation.

"Umm good thank you, it's a bit.."

"We're not splitting up, we're all going together or not at all." Matthew had suddenly burst out cutting through Michael's words. He looked shocked at his own nerve but looked up into Suzy's eyes. Suzy and Brad shared a glance while huffing in slight amusement.

"Don't worry, Dexter has told us all about you. We won't split you up," spoke Brad softly.

A calm chatter started between the six people and Matthew was becoming more and more calm about the whole process. The hands on the large metal clock spun slowly round, a soft ticking sound beating around the room. Penelope and Michael were chanting wildly about what they liked to do, and when the topic of how they came to be at the orphanage came Michael leapt into the long story, Penelope chirping in a few words every so often. Matthew was smiling now and just stared at the couple.

The balanced and chirpy conversation came to a slow halt and with a quick glance at the never ending clock, Dexter gave a formal clap of the hands.

"Right, that should do for today, you go and have lunch you three, I'll just finish up with the Taylor's."

"Goodbye children."

"Yes, good bye," called Suzy and Brad while Penelope and Michael have a short smile and Matthew a little wave. The rest of the day evaporated into a haze of excited chatter of what was to come about the Taylor's. all three children were now certain on going if Suzy and Brad wanted them and didn't quiver to start talking wildly of what life would be like with the Taylor's.

Anticipation and excitement reeked around the children's rooms and the next few days passed by slowly, Penelope, Michael and Matthew snapping their eyes to Margaret's office every five minutes, hoping and wishing for a message about the Taylors.

Finally, late on a Tuesday evening while the children were deep in a drawing competition, the timer ticking softly and Penelope's face looking panic stricken while Michael's very serious, Margaret's face peered softly around the door. She spoke only a few words.

"Children, could you come into my office for one second."

She left, glints of a long green dress flicking round the door. The ridgeway children were left staring fearfully but excitedly at each other, their eyes widening slowly into round almonds sized circles .

18
The Lion's Inn

THE SUN BURST from underneath the dark hills and trees while birds started to Twitter madly in a chorus of wonderful sound. All three children awoke, sprung out of bed and crossed to each other's room, grins wide on their tired flushed faces.

"What do you think we will do with them?"

"Oo, I don't know, something great, anyway let's get ready, they're coming in an hour." Michael said, turning around, panic sketched into his face as he rushed round, grabbing some clothes. Matthew and Penelope just sat silent watching Michael in confusion and almost pity.

He started to mumble softly, mostly to himself about what school books he should bring to show Susie and Brad.

"No, Michael, no books!" shouted them both, staring wildly at Michael.

"You're overthinking, let's just follow their lead,"
And with that, Penelope pounced up back to her room, snatching at her teddy off the perfectly made bed.

*   *   *

Coats on and ready, the children stood by the door, shuffling their feet impatiently whilst half listening to Margaret talking to Susie and Brad about her phone number and times they had to be back for. Susie emerged, wearing a cosy grey coat and Brad followed, slipping into his tweed jacket. They smiled hesitantly at the children who grinned back, Michael stepping on Penelope's foot in his eagerness to talk to Brad.

"Right, let's be off now." said Susie, taking Matthew's hand.

"Where are we going?" he asked.

"Let's keep it a surprise shall we Susie," Brad said just as Susie had opened her mouth to reply, "then it'll be more fun!"

It was nice walking on the pavement with people who weren't Sam, Sophie or Margaret and the children enjoyed themselves, even after their silent argument about who was to walk next to the kind hearted couple. They eventually agreed that Matthew would walk with Susie in front and the twins would walk with Brad just behind them, where they could ask all their questions about him being in the police force.

They turned off the pavement after a while and into an alleyway, which the children had never been before. Matthew would have normally felt uneasy, but with Susie holding his hand and talking at his side, and Brad's shoes clopping loudly just behind him, it didn't occur to him about the many dangers at all that could lurk in a dark place like this.

The small group wandered slowly into another alleyway, with a few small shops and some faded blue and red bunting crisscrossing down the rough, stone track. Two minutes passed and the three children's eyes were caught by a large lion's head sign hanging above their heads.

Suzy and Brad, without hesitation, headed confidently into a large pub named 'the Lions Inn' and the children, confused but excited, hurried in after. The pub was filled with old, vintage wood, and a huge wall of brick, a grand fireplace set into it, was placed heavily in the far end. Large tables with small metal chairs were scattered around the room and a soft, pleasant glow of faint yellow filled the corners of the light grey walls. It was a comfortable yet smart place that increased the children's excitement wildly. A small, blonde woman with a heart shaped face and a name tag attached to her shirt said, 'Louise' and a broad smile trotted happily towards them and led the Taylor's and the children towards a table just by the brick wall, uttering a few kind words of greeting. The children for once didn't fight over a seat and sat down staring amazed at the neat little table setting with a large menu tucked between the napkins.

"Right here we are, we've only been here once but it seemed lovely when we last came so we thought we would take you."

"Yes, I recommend the burgers!" Spoke Brad, leaning in to talk to the children.

"It's lovely, I mean look at this napkin. It's so white." Squealed Penelope while whipping up the piece of cloth and giving an approving look to Matthew.

"Yes, I can't wait."

A conversation commenced before Louise strolled back towards their small table.

"Right, what drinks would you like?"

"Umm, I'll have a beer."

"Yes, I'll have a glass of the Sauvignon Blanc."

"We will all have some lemonade, thank you," said Michael on behalf of the other two leaning forward towards the waitress, attempting at acting like a well mannered adult. The drinks came in tall, cloudy glasses and the children slurped them down very quickly. With this, the waitress stood with a small pad of paper.

"What about for the main?" she asked in a small chirp. Brad, Penelope and Matthew choose the cheese burger, Suzy picked the carbonara pasta and when it came to Michael, he asked,

"Now, am I allowed the classic burger but without the gherkins, tomatoes, mayonnaise and lettuce? If that's ok?" his voice trailed away timidly.

A swift smile came from the woman and she uttered perfect with a small rise of the eyebrows before strolling back towards the kitchens.

Fifteen minutes later, the food arrived, steaming hot and smelling delicious.

Penelope seized her burger and shoved it into her open mouth, the juice dribbling her chin as she chomped with her teeth covered in the brown meat, wiping her mouth clean of any burger juice smears with the back of her hand.

Michael winced and tried to divert Taylor's attention from Penelope onto himself so they would hopefully not see her doing what he would call a 'disgusting common thing'.

Matthew also chomped aggressively at his burger but Michael, quite annoyed at his siblings behaviour, now picked up his knife and fork and carefully, with his wrist bent and cutlery upright, slid his knife through a small chip before spiking a minuscule piece of potato onto his fork and placing it carefully in his mouth. He gave a quick glaze hoping for a comment on his manners but not came

For the first time, a silence occurred with the whole group deep in their huge platefuls of food. Michael almost looked overwhelmed at his plate and seemed to be measuring the size of his burger with his knife. A few minutes later, Suzy and Brad started chatting quietly of chores to do at home while Penelope whispered ever so softly to Michael.

"Score out of ten?"

"Yes, a strong eight and a half."

"Really, I felt a nine but you probably felt the portions were too large."

"Well, yes, you jolly know well I did, but that's a minor problem,"

Michael was slow to eat due to his careful cutting and measuring of food and when four plates lay clear with crumbs and sauce smeared across the white China, Michael started to pick up the pace and gauged a whole into his burger reaching halfway.

The plates were cleared and with a word to the Taylor's, Michael had assured them that he and his sibling were full and didn't need pudding. This comment, receiving murderous looks from the other two, the group waiting slightly on edge for the bill.

"Right, do you want to go splits?" called Michael once the bill had arrived, returning to his pompous adult like voice.

"What, no of course not," said Susie, giving a small chuckle.

"Yes, it's our treat." said Brad, whipping out a wallet and softly passing some notes into the short woman's hand. She took the money, she slipped it into her back pocket, and gave a small wave of farewell to the children.

A rambling walk took place as five full bellies traipsed slowly, bloated cheeks filling their faces.

"Right, we better say goodbye here, can we leave you to get in alright?"

"Yes definitely, thank you so much for lunch."

"Oh no, it was very nice to get to know you better."

"Yes, bye Penelope, Michael and Matthew." said Brad.

The party split and the children headed to the large white door, beaming at each other.

"Well that went well," said Michael in a business like way.

"Yes, they are very nice," babbled Matthew slightly skipping.

"And they remembered all of our names and let me tell you, that's a hardship,"

The frequent look of pure confusion but slight admiration was shared between the two boys as they all headed up the stairs splitting at the top into their separate rooms.

19
Belonging

FROST SHONE WHITE on the flaking wooden windowsill, reflecting the bright blue winters sky. The back garden lay slightly silver, a shade of green rippling through. The strands of grass tilted heavy, large frozen crystals of ice balancing precariously on top. A bright maroon curtain stretched open wildly, as a flash of blonde hair and a wide smile upon a slightly red face appeared, staring excitedly down onto the quiet, peaceful village, not yet bustling with the usual crowd of horse riders, cyclists and yoga mums yearning for a coffee. She took a glance at the first winter's frost and whipped out of sight.

Another room, sore to the eyes with green, camo-coloured walls, much to the dislike of Michael—he had seen this as very much the greatest plus of leaving, found a boy perched on his bed racking his mind back for anything else to pack. As he had packed two days ago, this position, sitting on the bed staring straight ahead, had occurred quite a lot.

As it was Tuesday, he was slightly annoyed that he was missing school, where he was almost certain they would learn about the Magna Carta, a subject he had greatly looked forward to but he supposed he would just have to catch up in his next school.

The shiny wooden bed frame beneath the bright white sheets creaked loudly as Michael jumped up, remembered he had already packed his toothbrush twice and sat back down again, slightly bored. The struggling silence was broken, however by a loud chorus of squawks and the wooden door slamming open, weakening the small hinges to reveal Penelope's peach coloured face. She slumped on the bed for a fraction of a second before jumping back up.

"Michael, today has come, we're moving!"

"I know, firstly you told me about a million times yesterday, and secondly I do have a brain."

Matthew clattered in next and bounded to them both, giving them an enormous hug. Michael returned the beaming smile this time and stood up, muttering constantly of all the packing he had done.

"Toothbrushes and toothpaste are done, clothes done, the cards given by Margaret, done" he said making unnecessary dramatic ticking gestures in the air while Penelope chirped in joining Michael in saying 'done'.

The suitcases were stuffed to the brim, clothes spilling out of Penelope's and Matthews, whilst Michaels was neatly packed, the folded shirts and trousers almost singing with smugness.

The decision that the children would move into the Taylor's had been decided not even two days ago, and the

Ridgeway children had been beside themselves with excitement, so alas, only Michael had thought of packing his things before 9:30 the previous night—unlike his siblings. Penelope had been most surprised, however, that Michael had waited a whole 30 minutes before starting to pack after they had been told they were going to move in with their beloved new family.

"Hurry up children!" A shout floated upstairs.

Penelope, who had been heaving her heavy bones and suitcase onto the landing outside her bedroom, quickened her pace. She ended up running on the spot, bent low, pushing madly at her suitcase before it crashed and banged down the stairs. A swift silence of embarrassment followed this as Penelope froze in shock and, feeling self-conscious, hurried down after rolling the bag.

Though the children didn't have many possessions on coming to the orphanage, their suitcases had been stuffed with double the things. Figures from shops, toys, sweets and more had been shoved hurriedly into Matthew's suitcases and he had spent several minutes heaving at the tiny, metal zip to shut the bag tight.

The bags were neatly stood side by side, carefully positioned by Michael so the suitcases were in rainbow and size order.

The children stood, waiting. Michaels wrist was rapidly swiping up and down while he constantly checked his watch while Matthew's head was full of dreadful thoughts that the Taylor's weren't coming.

"Right they should be here in precisely 27 seconds, are you ready?"

"Why but of course we are!" Said Penelope, giving her foot a sharp tap.

The door knocked, then opened and there stood the Taylor's, looking hardly less excited than the children. Dexter hurried in with Margaret and greeted the couple warmly.

"Right, children, I guess this is goodbye." Margaret said, slightly out of breath.

"Thank you so much, it's been wonderful."

"Thank you for coming, you will be missed greatly,"

"Yes, Mittens will miss you dreadfully, her favourites, by the look of it." Popped in Mrs Carmichael, having trotted hurriedly across the corridor, Mittens the cat just behind. The children gave a warm smile to the kind but slightly mad face before turning to Dexter.

"Thank you Dexter, you have found us a home."

"Ah, no problem, we got there in the end." He chuckled.

While Suzy and Brad sat there slightly awkwardly, Matthew ran up and hugged Margaret, who was almost knocked off her feet.

"Goodbye."

Margaret gave a weak smile and as the other two leant in to hug heras well, she patted their heads gently.

"Right, time for you to go, I'm sure we will meet again, hopefully not to take you back as you were too much work for the Taylors." she said, causing a series of chuckles from the children, the Taylor's and Margaret herself.

There was silence for a while before Susie started.

"Right, let's get your bags in the car shall we and then be off."

"Yes, there's a cake in the oven, sadly not made by me."

"Yes sir," Michael yelled, his hand shooting in a formal salute before grabbing at all three bags, dropping one, and walking on slightly embarrassed.

Matthew and Penelope gave one more admiring look towards Dexter, Margaret and Mrs Carmichael before walking out shouting a few goodbyes. Margaret lent forward and softly pressed the door shut.

"I am definitely going to miss those three."

"Yes but they looked very happy leaving."

"Anyway, a cup of tea Dexter?"

*   *   *

A sign hammered hard into the ground read 'Symonds Farm' in blue letters. The white washed thatch cottage stood alone in a sea of green gardens. The stuffed red car creaked slowly up the drive, groaning under all the suitcase's weight. The children's faces dotted the windows as they eagerly looked out onto their new home. Penelope shoved Matthew out of the way when they neared the house but he was too excited to care. They all spilled out of the car and grabbed their suitcases, the air buzzing with excitement.

They walked slowly towards the metal gate, their feet crunching at the deep cream coloured gravel, while their eyes revolved from side to side, taking in the beautiful farmhouse. Metal framed windows with tall flowers and roses strung across the pale white walls, a long brick wall carpeted thickly with ivy and a wide grassed lawn, white hoops stuck roughly into the ground stood in front of their mesmerized eyes. Beyond the lawn, stood five large apple trees, small circles and large green leaves dangling and waving in the soft winters breeze. The children strolled through a brick arch way, just behind Susie and Brad, before exclaiming wildly at the croquet balls and mallets.

"Oh I can't wait to play!"

The crowd quietly stood by the door, Brad ruffling into his pocket before pulling out a small key.

The key turned in the green door's lock, revealing a cosy kitchen before a golden dog leapt up the children's legs.

"Get down Teaser!" Said Brad, not really meaning it.

"Oh is that your dog!" Penelope said in excitement, leaning down to stroke the pretty thing, "He's wonderful."

"Thank you Penelope," said Susie, "except for the fact that she's indeed a girl!" She chuckled. "Well, come into your new home treasures!"

"Yes, get you all warm and out of the cold, and we can show you your new rooms!"

They bounded inside, the suitcase bashing against their ankles in the children's haste to get inside.

The house's interior was nothing as grand as the Ridgeway Manor, but somehow, the children didn't seem to care. Long slabs of wood lined the walls, faded clouds of mud set into them, a waft of dust waving into the air. Michael spared a thought for the dust at the cellar and slightly shuddered. A smaller island than the one at Ridgeway Manor stood in the middle of the room and grubby cream coloured cupboards lay haphazardly around the wall, making way for a large aga set into the wall. Susie strolled forward, giving a quick tour of the room before perching on a window seat while looking round into the garden.

"I can show you the garden in a second but before that shall we head to your bedrooms and let you settle in?"

They all trooped upstairs, the cream carpet fluffy beneath their feet as they climbed the steep staircase. At the top of the stairs, a large platform arose. Two smaller steps of stairs were found, leading in different directions. The one closest to the right was used, and the children followed their new guardians down a corridor.

"Here is your room Matthew!" Said Susie, pushing open a white door with a green M on it. She indicated further down the corridor. "Those two rooms are yours Penelope and Michael." She said smiling. The three rooms were right next to each other and large but cosy with big, comfy beds and long rugs filling the wooden floors. Penelope flung her bag onto the bed but didn't make herself too comfortable, too eager to explore the garden and not so interested in lying on her bed.

They leapt out of the door wildy and ran up the garden, Teaser yapping at their heels. The back garden was yet larger here, with trees dotted here and there and a large trampoline set at the back. The children's eyes fell onto the metal frame and bouncing material and quickened their pace before leaping onto the trampoline and jumping higher and higher. Brad and Susie followed at a slower pace chatting animatedly and stopped to watch the children.

Lunch came next and the children were found perched at the island, knives and forks grabbed in their hands. Susie placed three plates with large bacon sandwiches bursting with ketchup before the children and being careful to swiftly ask if they were allowed to start digging into the sandwiches.

"We've never had bacon before, it's jolly nice," munched Penelope between mouthfuls.

"Well we love it, me and Brad, I mean. I thought we would have ice cream for pudding."

"Oo, yes that sounds delightful," said Matthew shoving his last mouthful into his mouth. Brad walked in swiftly, his phone in his hand and grabbed at a sandwich.

"Thanks dear, these look great, have you played croquet yet you three?"

"No, not yet but I have a feeling I will be pretty good at it."

"Oh no, I better watch out."

A loud knock at the door interrupted the new family's game of Racing Demon and Susie heaved up and moved swiftly towards the front door. The great piece of wood swung open, revealing a short woman dressed in dungarees and a large smile. She had short brown hair and eyes that shone like the ocean.

"Hello Pat!" Said Susie in a surprised and welcoming voice. Everyone stopped playing cards and craned their necks to see this visitor better.

"Hello Mrs Taylor!" Pat said in a harsh country accent. "I've got some nice juicy eggs for ya! Straight from me chicks they are!" She brought her hand to mouth and said in an audible whisper, "I don't chatter, you know me, but I hear wedding bells near the Anderson Household, there might be a bump forming on Miss Ann soon enough. Their parents will be pleased, just telling me last week that those two should better get a move on.

Susie rolled her eyes and sighed. "Oh Pat! Last week you thought Mr Lawson was having a wee in mongolia and it turned out he was skiing in Austria. Anyway, how are the chickens?"

"You have chickens?" Asked Matthew timidly.

Pat did a double take when she saw the children and Brad sitting round the table.

"Ahh, these must be the wee children yer adopted." She said, looking at Susie who nodded.

"Anyway," she looked at Matthew, "I raised them from when they were wee chicks I did! You three can come and feed me if ya fancy it!"

"Can we Susie? Tomorrow morning?" Asked Michael, suddenly excited about the prospect of going 'outside' which had never happened in his life.

"Oh yes of course dear! I'm sure Pat would appreciate the help!"

"I sure as well could mind!" Said Pat and then turned whilst saying, "best be off now, the lambs are gonna want a feeding."

She thrust a box of eggs into Susie's hands and strolled out of the door, closing it behind her.

"She seemed nice!" Said Penelope.

"Oh yes, she's been our next for neighbour for years! Brings round eggs most mornings!"

"Yes and they're always free range!"

*   *   *

The children cracked on with a game of croquet, grabbing at the big, wooden mallets and smashing at the heavy balls. Matthew took red while penelope and Matthew took black and blue. The game started and Matthew looked as if he was in a winning position. However the game turned and Penelope and Matthew started to join forces in taking down the smug and smiling face of Michael.

"Matthew, why are you croqueting me? We are working together!"

"Sorry but I need to get to these hoops to croquet Michael."

"Well you could have told me," Penelope asid turning around annoyed.

Two minutes later, a loud clunk came followed by a cheer and a growl signalling the game ending and Michael winning.

"Oh darn, I thought I was catching you up,"

The children were just turning into the door when they heard a crunch of gravel and a patter of feet as Susie ran out muttering to the children

"Oh, I'm so sorry for not telling you but my parents are coming to meet you, is that ok?"

"Yes, it will be nice to have grandparents,"

"Grandparents, this is more than I bargained for!" Penelope squealed in horror.

"Penelope, Grandparents means more presents at Christmas," Michael whispered softly.

"Oh well, that's better, I knew there must be a positive."

The children rushed outside, through the gateway onto the crackling drive and rushed to the big wooden gate pulling and heaving it open to make way for the large car.

Two old people, broad smiles on tehri wrinkled faces drove in, and then walked slowly and gradually to the children, a mound full of presents in the smaller lady's hand.

"Children, how nice to see you, what are your names?"

"I'm Michael, and these two are Penelope and Matthew," again said Michael taking charge.

"Penelope, lovely," said the elder lady, a slight edge of surprise and sarcasm in her voice. Susie welcomed the two in chatting to them wildly on the journey to get the children and once inside seated them down for a cup of coffee.

"These gifts are for you children," said the older man, Susie's father, passing the pile to Matthew whose knees buckled slightly under the weight. Penelope headed to the door, a scratching sound awakening her ears and opened it to reveal a blonde labrador who bounded towards Susie's mother.

"Whos dog is this,"

"Oh, that's ours, Nutmeg"

"Nutmeg, what a nice name."

"I've never seen so many dogs in one house," said Matthew

"Yes, we have just come from an orphanage and now we're in a dog pound." Chuckled penelope.

"You two, pull yourselves together, it's only two." Whispered Michael, annoyed, who at that moment was working hard to think of a way to join in on the conversation. The afternoon drowned on slowly, the children repeatedly bending forwards to grab a cake, and when finally the large, beige car backed slowly out of the driveway, the wrinkled and blue eyed faces of their new grandparents smiling weekly while giving a small wave, the children, as well as Susie and Brad, were deeply tired.

A quiet and uneventful supper of shepherd's pie followed, one of the children's favourites, and little chat occurred, the sound of clinking glasses and cutlery filling the cosy kitchen. The sun was down and as the clock hit eight, Susie softly wafted them to their bedroom in order to get dressed into their pyjamas. Penelope was found, so often these days, spread out on her bed. She thought and the only thing that seemed right as this moment in time was to wander off to Michael's room

She walked down the quiet corridor on the pale blue rug into Michael's room, thinking up an excuse to tell him about interrupting his private space. She slowly slotted into the room and sank down on his bed, beside her brother who was deep in his favourite book, war and peace.

"Yes Penelope?" Michael asked without looking up.

"How did you know it was me?"

"I wonder…"

"I'm so happy we came here Michael," said Penelope, choosing to ignore her brother's comment.

"So am I Penny." Michael shut his book with a snap and stared hard at his sister. "Penelope? You don't miss the old -"

"Stop Michael. Just forget about that. Live in the moment."

"Oh alright Pen. Well, good night."

"Good night Michael."

Penelope left the room, went through the corridor, passing Susie, who was on the way to Matthew's bedroom, and into her own room where she flopped onto her bed. It had been an exhausting day.

*   *   *

"Right shall we get you off to bed Matthew, would you like some warm milk?"

Susie was tucking Matthew in—a strange sensation for him as none of his old parents had ever done this.

"Oo, yes please, I love it here, thank you so much"

"Oh, that's quite alright, you're the best thing that has happened to me and Brad." said Susie in a warm and soft voice, whilst she smoothed his blankets covered in a watercolour type pattern.

"If you need anything, you can always come down, or into our bedroom, we're just down the corridor."

Susie hurried downstairs, her feet padding on the landing until she reached the kitchen as Matthew settled more comfortably into his bed and pulled the thick sheets up to his neck, listening to the comforting sound of the microwave beeping as Susie heated up some milk for him.

She soon returned, giving him a blue snoopy mug and told him a bit about her childhood, while Matthew sat, half unright, and listened, sipping slowly at the milk, gripping the small mug. Susie gave him a quick kiss on the forehead after tucking him gently into the large bed and crept off, closing the door quietly before tip-toeing gently down the creaking corridor, waving goodnight to the other two.

*   *   *

The house was dark and silent apart from the soft yellow light of the kitchen where Susie and Brad were downstairs, enjoying a few crisps and a drink each, to quietly celebrate the start of their new life.

"I'm so glad we did this!"

"I am too Susie." Said Brad, clinking Susie's glass softly.

"Brad what—" began Susie, but what she was about to say Brad never knew, as there was a sharp knock on the door.

Susie hurried over, wondering about the package she'd ordered earlier.

She held her fist on the door knob, twisted the metal handle and heaved the door open.

There stood a woman, half her body in shadow, her hands clasped, rings clinking softly. Her face was pale and thinned, her hair in a bird's nest but there was an unmistakable air about the way she held her head.

There stood, straight and tall on the worn stone pathway of Symonds Farm House…

Caroline Ridgway.

To be continued...

Acknowledgments

J. K. Rowling's Harry Potter, for endless inspiration;

Stephen Fry, for voicing our dark afternoons of no ideas with interesting and exciting audio books;

Our families, for the support and ideas that helped us so much;

Dr Gardener of the Abingdon School Library, for contacts and help that was very much needed;

About the Authors

Tom Lawson, born in 2006, grew up in a country village in England from birth, while his cousin, Maddy Anderson, born in 2005, moved to Abu Dhabi when she was three. Ten years later, Maddy moved back to England, keen to be closer to her loved ones. Tom Lawson and Maddy Anderson are new writers; at the age of 13 and 14 they started developing this book word by word, character by character. Those young minds thought up a tale of three children and spilled it onto the page. Ransom and Revenge has impacted them on a scale neither of them expected.

Printed in Great Britain
by Amazon